THE OTHER FATHER CHRISTMAS

Other books by Serena Holly

The Marvellous Granny Jinks and Me

The Marvellous Granny Jinks and Me: Animal Magic!

Books by Priscilla Mante

The Dream Team: Jaz Santos vs the World

The Dream Team: Charligh Green vs the Spotlight

The Dream Team: Naomie Mensa vs the Future

Football's Hidden History

Books by Jasmine Richards

The Unmorrow Curse

The Myth Keeper

SERENA HOLLY

THE OTHER FATHER CHRISTMAS

Illustrated by
SHAHAB SHAMSHIRSAZ

STORYMIX BOOKS

STORYMIX BOOKS

First published in the UK by Storymix Books in 2025
Storymix Limited, The Wenta Business Centre,
Colne Way, Watford, Hertfordshire, WD24 7ND

STORYMIX
BOOKS

Email: info@storymix.co.uk
Website: www.storymixbooks.com
Follow us on social media @storymixstudio
Reader resources for this book are available on our website.

Text by Priscilla Mante and Jasmine Richards writing as Serena Holly
Cover and inside illustrations by Shahab Shamshirsaz
Text and illustrations © Storymix Limited, 2025

Paperback ISBN: 978–1–916–74772–2
Hardback ISBN: 978–1–068–16650–1
Ebook ISBN: 978–1–068–16651–8

A CIP catalogue record for this book is
available from the British Library

Text design by Becky Chilcott
With thanks to Fox & Ink Books for publishing services

Printed in the UK

1 3 5 7 9 8 6 4 2

For all who dream of a

magical Christmas – PM

For my grandparents and all the

Windrush grandparents – JR

For my dearest Giovanni – SS

'**JINGLE BELLS, JINGLE BELLS, JINGLE ALL** the waaaaaaaaaay!'

I stretched out the last word as I heaved a gigantic box of Christmas decorations onto the kitchen table.

Dad took up the song as he mopped the kitchen floor. '*Oh, what fun it is to ride in a one-horse open sleigh . . .*' He shimmied over to Mum and winked. '*HEY!*'

Mum laughed, spun away from the jollof rice cooking on the stove, and grabbed a nearby

wooden spoon to use as a microphone. '*Dashing through the snow . . .*'

I glanced over at Gramps, waiting for his deep soulful voice to take the next line, but he just sat there, looking glum, sipping his cocoa tea as Mum and Dad carried on singing. It was as if he hadn't heard us at all.

'Countdown to Christmas starts now,' I said to him gently.

Gramps slouched further in his seat and gazed out of the window at the falling snow. I inhaled the steam coming from his BEST GRANDAD EVER mug. His cocoa tea smelled of chocolate, milk, nutmeg and cinnamon – exactly the way he and Gran liked it.

'Gramps, are you OK?' I asked.

'No, Mikey Boy.' Gramps turned to me with big, sad eyes. 'Missing your gran badly today – Claudette loved the snow.'

I caught Mum and Dad sharing a look. I missed

Gran too. We all did, but we were also worried about Gramps. He had changed so much since she died and, even though he moved in with us after the funeral, he felt more distant than ever. I guess I missed *him* too. The way he used to be.

'Gramps, do you remember this?' I dug into the box of decorations and pulled out a bent yellow star made out of cardboard. It twirled on its little string. Maybe it would bring him back, even only for a moment.

Gramps nodded. 'Of course! You made that in nursery. It was one of Claudette's favourite decorations.'

I touched the star and it felt rough beneath my fingers. 'I don't know why Gran thought it was so amazing. The edges aren't even straight.'

'Ah, your gran knew a true artist when she saw one.' His eyes were watery all of a sudden.

My throat felt tight. We missed Gran every

day, but today was the first time I realised how lonely Christmas might feel for Gramps. I needed to see him smile again.

I reached for the silliest thing in the box. 'Hey, Gramps – it's Cheeky Santa!'

I held up a red-and-white ornament in the shape of Santa's head. We'd bought it at the Christmas market in town last year because its silly expression had made us laugh.

Going to the Christmas market with Gran and Gramps was a Merriman tradition. We'd buy gifts, wander past stalls piled with festive treats from around the world, like spicy German sausages, sweet pastries and glistening bottles of red Jamaican sorrel. We'd try all the samples as well, so we got a taste of everything.

Last year, we went on the Christmas Big Wheel for the first time. Seeing Liverpool lit up below us felt like magic. That was just weeks before everything changed and Gran got ill.

'Good thing you're *our* Santa and not this guy,' I said, giving the Cheeky Santa bauble a little shake, making the bell inside it jangle. 'Not sure he could organise a grotto as great as yours this year.'

I felt a burst of pride thinking of Gramps in the grotto. He'd been the Father Christmas at Toxteth Community Centre for as long as I could remember. The grotto was *his* thing, and setting it up was the most important moment of the Merriman year. Gramps said it was his job to bring Christmas magic to town, as the real Santa had enough on his plate and the way Gramps said it made you really believe he could.

Gramps shifted in his seat. 'Go on – what else can you find?' he asked.

I reached deeper into the box and felt something cool and crinkly. Tinsel! As I pulled the tinsel free, something else came with it. I blinked. *Oh no.* Of all the decorations, it had to be this one.

Caught in the loops of tinsel was the angel that we always put at the top of the tree. The one Gramps had made to look like Gran.

It was one of my favourite family Christmas stories, actually. I'd only been a baby then. Gramps said that he'd spent years trying to find an angel that looked like Gran – because she was his angel – but he'd had no luck, so he made one himself in his shed. He carved and painted for days, giving the angel her deep-brown skin, round cheeks, and coiled black and grey hair tucked into a perfectly neat bun. Gran-Angel had delicate wings and a sparkling silver dress that Gramps had sewn by hand. He had surprised her with it that Christmas Eve.

The tears stinging my eyes made the angel seem as though it was shimmering. Great, now me and Gramps were *both* teary. I brushed my sleeve over my face.

Just then, Dad started crashing around in the cupboards, pulling out mixing bowls and baking tins. I think he was making all that noise on purpose.

'Hey, Mikey, what day is it today?' he called over, grinning in that bright red jumper of his, which had Santa's legs sticking out of a chimney.

'Er . . . Tree-Decorating Day?' I said. Because the first Saturday of December was always Tree-Decorating Day.

He gave me a little wink. '*And* Christmas Cake Day.'

'No, it's not,' I said, frowning. 'Gran always made the cake in the *middle* of December.'

The recipe for Gran's famous Jamaican fruit cake with icing had been passed down through

her family for generations, and she only ever made it on the second weekend of December. I felt annoyed that Dad had got it wrong.

'Let's be spontaneous, Mikey. Come on!' Dad said. 'It's good to change things up.'

He started grabbing ingredients from the cupboards and setting them out on the counter. 'We'll make two Christmas cakes. One for us, one for the homeless shelter. And we'll take some oxtail stew too, like Mum used to. She'd be proud, wouldn't she, Dad?'

Gramps opened his mouth to reply but couldn't seem to find any words.

'Let's put some music on,' Dad said, sounding extra cheery. He switched on the radio and music burst out of the speaker. It was Donny Hathaway singing 'This Christmas'.

I only knew it was Donny Hathaway because

Gran used to play that song on repeat at Christmas time. Dad let out a quiet groan. I winced, expecting Gramps to be even sadder with this song playing, but he gave us a small smile instead.

'Claudette always said I had a voice like Donny's . . . Love makes a fool of us all, I guess,' he murmured, then he started humming along.

With the music playing, me and Dad measured out the ingredients – dried fruit, grape juice (no rum), butter, brown sugar, eggs, vanilla, flour, mixed spice, cinnamon. Then we set to work mixing it all up. Soon, there were smudges of flour on the wall *and* the floor tiles, and splats of batter all over the counter.

'You two!' Mum put her hands on her hips. 'We've just cleaned the kitchen. I suppose you think magic elves are going to come in the night and tidy this up?'

I grinned. 'Actually, Gramps, do you need help

at the grotto this year? I could be your *elf-er*. You know. Elf-helper?'

Gramps let out a quiet chuckle. Not his thunderous old laugh, but it was still good to hear. 'Kind of you to offer, Mikey . . .'

I could sense there was a 'but' coming.

'. . . *but* I'm not sure I'm up to it this year.'

Dad dropped the electric mixer. Bits of cake batter flew everywhere before the whisk stuttered to a stop.

'But you're the Other Father Christmas!' Dad cried. 'You're the Toxteth Santa! The—'

'I can't do it,' Gramps interrupted. 'Not . . . not without my Claudette.' He sounded so sad.

Dad rushed over to Gramps and hugged him tightly.

'We all miss her, Dad,' he whispered. 'We always will, but she wouldn't want you to give the grotto up. She loved it there, and she loved seeing you as Father Christmas even more.'

I picked up a wooden spoon and carried on stirring in the cake ingredients, thinking about how Gran would nudge and wink at me so I'd remember to make a wish at just the right moment, when the last ingredient had gone in and the cake batter was fully mixed. It was the same tradition every time we made the cake together.

I watched Gramps as I moved the spoon round and round the mixing bowl, and I made my Christmas wish.

The festive music abruptly cut off, mid-song.

'*Put down your mince pies and dust off your jingle bells,*' the radio host said, sounding rather breathless. '*News just in . . . Santa is about to make a very important announcement!*'

I RACED TO THE FRONT ROOM AND TURNED ON
the TV. If Santa was making an announcement,
I needed to see it. Every single channel seemed to
have it on.

Mum, Dad and Gramps joined me and we
stared at the screen in disbelief. There in front of
a snowy forest was Santa with his bright red suit
and full white beard, behind a microphone stand
shaped like a shiny present.

'No way! It's the real Santa Claus,' Dad
breathed. 'And are those . . . elves next to him?'

'Santa's got to be speaking from the North Pole,' said Mum. 'Look at all that snow!'

Gramps didn't move a muscle.

Santa leaned into a red-and-white-striped microphone. 'Dear children and adults around the world,' he said, his voice deep and warm. 'I have an announcement to make.' He paused, then took a deep breath. 'I am retiring.'

Gasps rang out. Mine was the loudest.

'It has been the honour of my life to serve as Santa, or St Nick or Father Christmas or even "that jolly guy in the red suit",' he went on. 'Over the years, I have witnessed your joys and your kindnesses and your triumphs.' He dipped his head, solemn now. 'But times are changing and even Santas grow weary. And so I must hang up my boots.'

'WHAT?' I burst out. Santas don't retire! No Santa meant . . . no Christmas. Right? I bit my lip, hoping this was all some kind of joke.

In a second, he'd laugh and wink and shout, 'Got you!'

Instead, Santa raised a hand, as if he could hear us all panicking.

'Before I retire,' he said, 'I will appoint a new Santa. Just as I was chosen long ago. This new Santa will be kind and selfless, with a true understanding of what this season truly means.'

I glanced at Gramps, who was staring at the TV, his mouth hanging open, and I thought about my wish. I turned back to the screen and Santa smiled, the soft skin around his eyes crinkling with warmth. I gasped. It felt as though Santa was staring right at me and knew what I was thinking.

'The search for the next Santa begins today and applications will be open for a very short amount of time,' Santa said. 'Please read the terms and conditions posted outside in your villages, towns and cities to find out how to apply. I will be selecting five Santa's Hopefuls

to take part in a series of challenges, designed to test their ingenuity and bravery, and the strength of their Christmas spirit. The competition will be held here in Christmasland, or the North Pole, as some of you call it.' Santa waved a gloved hand at his surroundings.

'Time is of the essence,' he continued. 'The new Santa will take the *reins* this very Christmas.' Santa pulled out a scroll. 'The deadline for applications is 3 p.m. today *wherever* you are in the world – time is stretchy in Christmasland. How else do you think I deliver all those presents in one night?' he said with a wink. 'The chosen Santa's Hopefuls will also be announced by the end of the day.'

I frowned. How was Santa going to look at all the applications, select the candidates, oversee a bunch of challenges *and* train someone in time? There were only twenty-four more sleeps till Christmas. Time must be *really* stretchy in Christmasland.

On-screen, Santa tucked the scroll under his arm. 'Ho ho ho! May the best Santa win!'

With that, he stepped away from the microphone and the TV went back to the programme that was on before.

'What a wow,' Dad said, shaking his head as he muted the TV. 'This can't be actually happening, can it?'

'I suppose he had to retire eventually,' said

Gramps. 'And it's nice that Santa's announcing the competition. For all we know, a new Father Christmas might've been appearing every few decades, looking exactly like the old one, and we've been none the wiser.'

I couldn't help but think that Gramps would make a great Father Christmas – after all, he'd been our Toxteth Santa for years.

'Whoa! Look – it's wild out there already,' Mum said, peering out of the window. 'I bet everyone's going to apply!'

'Can I go out and see?' I asked, though I was already stuffing my arms into my puffer jacket.

'The answer's yes,' she called after me as I flung the front door open and raced outside. 'Just in case you were wondering.'

People were gathered around every lamp post and tree trunk on our street, the snow on the ground turning to grey slush from all the trampling feet.

'OK, the poster on this tree says we have to *film* our applications,' one person said nearby. 'Quick! Someone get my phone!'

'Ooh, I'm a nervous flyer,' said a dad with a baby in a sling. 'D'you think it'll be different if I'm in a sleigh, though?'

I stood on tiptoe trying to see the poster.

'Excuse me, can I take a look?' I asked, but no one took any notice.

The crowds were so tightly packed that I couldn't find a gap to squeeze into, and I kept getting jostled out of the way. Giving up, I stood back and noticed that some people were filming themselves already for their applications, posing with Christmas props. I couldn't blame them. Santa did say time was of the essence!

Two doors down, I noticed Ms Pudding, who was a teaching assistant at my school. She was dressed up in a shimmering green sequinned top and was beaming at a man in slippers, who was

recording her on a phone. She adjusted her red hat, which had a squashed Christmas pudding balanced on top of it.

'Ready . . . steady . . . ACTION!' the man said.

Ms Pudding yanked the Christmas pudding from her hat and took a huge bite.

'Delithious,' she said, her mouth full. She grimaced and continued to chew. 'Ho ho ho! Pudding by name, pudding by nature! And that's why I am the perfect San—'

She started coughing, spraying raisins everywhere. One pinged off the man's glasses.

Ms Pudding didn't miss a beat, though. 'Let's go again, Paul – or shall we try it with a mince pie this time?' She spat out another raisin. 'Yuck! I *hate* Christmas pudding!'

Paul shrugged. 'I don't know, love, but my toes are getting cold.'

'Hey, Ms Pudding,' I called out. 'You're applying to be Santa then?'

'That's right, Mikey! I certainly am,' Ms Pudding replied, brushing the crumbs off herself. She peered at me and said, 'Actually, could you stand right there and look at me like you're really pleased to see me?'

I stood awkwardly and Paul started filming again.

'Ho ho ho,' said Ms Pudding, smiling at the camera and then over at me. 'Lo! 'Tis a lovely child eager to partake in Christmas joy! Merry Christmas, young man. Here, have a Christmas pudding on me!'

She threw the rest of her pudding at me, but it came too fast and hit me smack on the forehead.

'OWWW!' I cried.

'You can cut that last bit out, Paul,' said Ms Pudding quickly. 'And, er . . . sorry, Mikey.'

I rubbed my forehead and looked around, hoping the crowds around the lamp posts would have thinned out by now.

'URGH!' yelled our next-door neighbour Freddie.

I looked up. At least I *think* it was Freddie – all I could see were his legs sticking out of his chimney!

'Yes, Fred!' his wife was saying, who was also on the roof, recording him. 'Santa's gonna love this! Sing "When Santa Got Stuck Up the Chimney" one more time and we'll be good to go.'

'Don't just stand there, Marjorie,' came a muffled voice from inside the chimney. 'HELP!'

As I peered upwards at Marjorie and Freddie, something glittery caught my eye. A shimmery flicker in the air to my left.

It was a poster! The sheet floated to the pavement, flipping and spinning as if it had a mind of its own. I ran after it as it danced through the air, before it smacked itself onto a lamp post. I gasped when I reached it. An actual magical poster straight from Christmasland!

It was a bit crumpled and damp, but it glowed and sparkled softly. Then I read it, and a warm, buzzy, tingly feeling shot right through me.

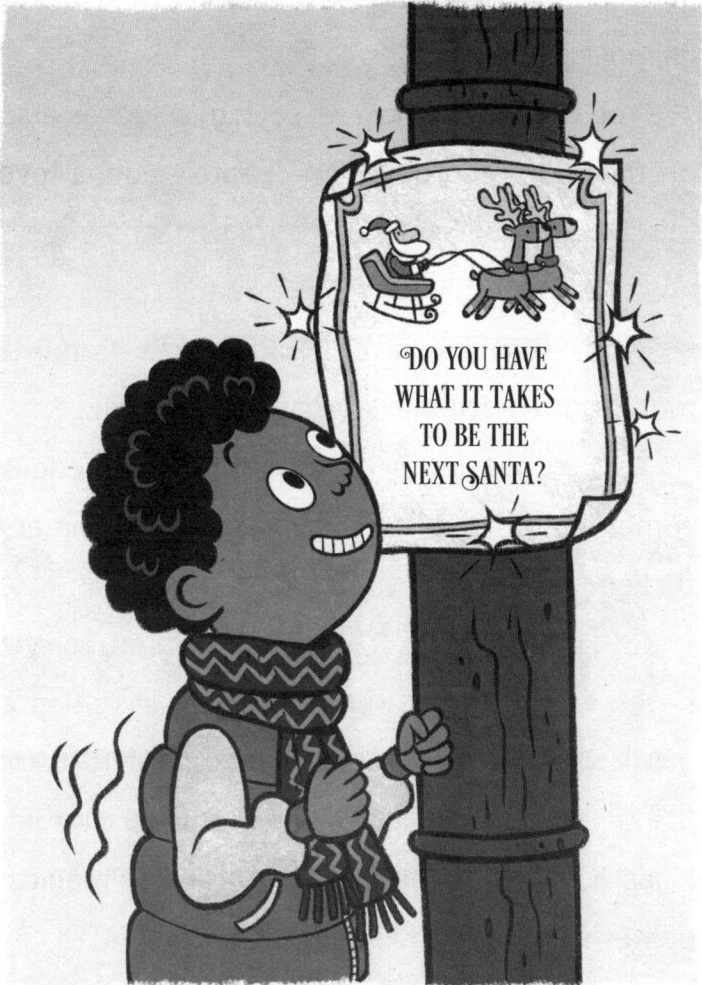

DO YOU HAVE WHAT IT TAKES TO BE THE NEXT SANTA?

3

THE POSTER SHIMMERED EVEN MORE
brightly and the words changed.

THE SANTA SEARCH RULES

Send a short video of yourself to www.thesantasearch.com by 3 p.m. today, explaining why you would make a great Santa. This must be a recent video and you must submit this video yourself.

You can be based anywhere in the world
but must be happy to travel for work.

You can be any gender but you must be over
40 years old. Life experience is essential.

If you are chosen as a Santa's Hopeful,
you may bring a helper to assist you during the
selection process. Children are welcome.

You must like to fly.

You must like wearing red with
a white faux-fur trim.

It helps if you are partial to mince pies
or cookies, and small glasses of milk.

You MUST believe in magic.

And in really small print at the bottom:

The new Santa will be selected from those
who have completed all assigned challenges
and demonstrated adherence to the rules of
the Santa Search. The new Santa must reflect
the values of the role in conduct, character
and spirit throughout the course of
the competition.

I knew just the person for the job. I grabbed
the poster and rushed back home.

'What've you got there, Mikey?' Dad asked as I kicked off my trainers in the front hallway.

'Err, nothing,' I said, clutching the poster close to my chest. 'Working on a project. That's all!'

I raced upstairs before he could ask any more questions and shut myself in my room.

My hands trembled with excitement as I read the poster again. Santa's words twinkled at me like an invitation.

You MUST believe in magic.

Magic was real. *Father Christmas was real.* And the job description? It described Gramps to a tee, but would he be up for applying?

I swept a mound of comic books off my desk and found my tablet hiding under a pile of half-finished homework. I turned it on and crept back downstairs.

Gramps was watching news coverage of the Santa Search, sipping another mug of cocoa tea.

I sprang into action.

'Hey, Gramps,' I said, doing my best to sound super casual as I rested the tablet on the bookshelf. 'I was thinking . . . you'd be perfect for this Santa job, you know.'

Gramps blinked at me. 'Oh no, Mikey Boy. There's no way! I'm not going to apply.'

'Yeah. Of course. Silly idea,' I mumbled. But, inside, I knew it wasn't silly at all. Gramps applying to be the next Santa was *meant to be*. How else could you explain Santa announcing his retirement right after I'd made my wish? And who knows . . . ? Maybe Gramps would even get the job! He'd be brilliant at it.

Secretly, I hit the record button on my tablet. It was the only way. I mean, Gramps didn't even want to be Father Christmas at the local grotto this year. He said he didn't want to be the real Santa either . . . but what if I applied for him . . . ?

'Gramps,' I said, 'would you say that Christmas is the most magical time of year?'

'Without doubt,' Gramps said, still watching the telly. 'But . . . but it can be hard for people as well.'

I nodded, then said, 'And, erm, wouldn't you agree that the colour red suits you? And you do like mince pies and glasses of milk?'

Gramps laughed and turned to me, giving me a funny look. 'What's all this about, Mikey?'

'It's for a school project,' I blurted out. 'We've got to find out what our families think about Christmas.'

Gramps only nodded and took another sip of his tea.

Phew.

'My teacher, Mr Beavin, told me it was best to record our interviews, so it'll be easier for us to write notes for our presentations,' I said, and I was surprised at how easily the lie slipped out.

I picked up the tablet. The footage I had so far was worse than Brussels sprouts. I thought

of our neighbour Freddie who'd been told to sing carols with his feet sticking out the chimney. People were bringing their A game and I had to try a different tactic to get Gramps to stand out from everyone else.

'I was wondering, Gramps,' I began, pointing the tablet's camera lens at him, 'what was your first Christmas in Liverpool like after you moved here from Jamaica?'

Gramps raised his eyebrows. 'Well, it was cold.' He gave a dramatic shiver. 'And new. And very different. I was sad about leaving my grandparents, and nervous as well, to make the trip on the plane alone. I remember being so excited about joining my parents here – they'd worked really hard to set up a home for us in England like so many who came over as part of the Windrush generation.'

He sighed. 'But I didn't really know them that well before I got here. Back then, they were just

the people who sent a barrel of exciting stuff every once in a while. I did love opening those barrels, though. It was like Christmas every time one came. The Family Circle tin of biscuits was my favourite.' He smiled at the memory. 'I arrived at Christmas time, you know. I was eleven years old, not much older than you are now.'

Now this was better! I held my breath, hoping he'd go on to tell the story about the first time he saw snow and how he tried to keep it from melting in his bedroom. But Gramps seemed to run out of steam. He went quiet and turned his attention back to the TV.

I sighed. Then again, Gramps had never been the biggest talker. That was always Gran's job. She said he was a 'man of action', but ever since she died, he'd not been taking much action or done much talking.

Carefully, I zoomed in on the framed newspaper article above his head.

TOXTETH TIMES

MR AND MRS CLAUS BRING THE CHRISTMAS SPIRIT TO OUR COMMUNITY

Once again, Curtis and Claudette Merriman have made Christmas the most wonderful time of the year for everyone in our community. Their inclusive grotto at the Toxteth Community Centre runs every December, welcoming all. There's always a smile, a small gift and plenty of food and drink for everyone and anyone in need. The Merrimans truly understand the meaning of Christmas and they deliver it to Toxteth year after year.

'It's kind of amazing that you're known around here as the Other Father Christmas,' I said. 'People love you like they love the real Santa.'

'I don't know about that, Mikey,' Gramps said with a snort.

'Gramps, can you remind me how you and Gran ended up in the paper?'

'I think your mum wrote to them. They were looking for community heroes or something like that. Claudette was so excited. Said we'd finally made the big time. She was a joker, your gran.'

'I love that photo of you and Gran, all dressed up,' I said, swinging the camera back to him. He was staring at the article now, his eyes full of something soft and far away.

When he spoke, it was barely above a whisper. 'Yeah. Festive cheer was never far away back then. Bringing the community together, making it fun for the little ones, spreading a bit of magic . . . It really was special. But with Claudette

gone . . .' He swallowed. 'This Christmas will look very different because I feel different. I'm not the same person I was, Mikey.'

I lowered the tablet and stopped recording.

'That's OK, Gramps,' I told him, running over to give him a hug. 'It's my turn to make Christmas special now,' I said under my breath.

I knew my old Gramps was still in there somewhere and that he loved Christmas. I just had to help him remember that.

4

I TRUDGED UP TO MY ROOM, THINKING HARD.
Right now, the video I'd just recorded was full
of reasons why Gramps should *not* to be chosen
for the job of Santa. I flopped onto my bed
and scrolled through old photos and videos of
Merriman Christmases on my tablet.

I grinned at a video of Gramps serving brown
stew chicken at the shelter. Gramps and Gran
welcoming visitors to the Toxteth Community
Grotto. A recording of me and Gran baking
her fruit cake, while Gramps sang one of his

Christmas mash-up songs in the background with his deep voice: '*Brown reindeer in the ring, tra la la la la!*'

If only Santa could've seen how Gramps used to bring the whole neighbourhood together and have us all laughing and celebrating Christmas.

I sat bolt upright. Maybe that was it. Maybe I could use the old videos for the application!

I walked to my desk and carefully smoothed out the magical poster. OK, so maybe it was against the rules to apply without Gramps's permission. And maybe these videos weren't exactly what you'd call *recent*. But it wasn't breaking the rules exactly . . . More like *bending* them. *Really* bending them. But it was for a good cause.

I nodded to myself and started dragging clips and photos showing Gramps in full Santa mode into a new file on the tablet. Images and music

layered together with today's interview. A proper nice video. Half an hour later, it was ready.

I guess this would be like one of Mum and Dad's Christmas pranks. They always pretended to forget presents and then surprised each other with big, beautifully wrapped gifts on Christmas morning. This was my Christmas surprise for Gramps.

I took a deep breath and logged on to www.thesantasearch.com. Then I tapped the bright red SUBMIT APPLICATION button.

There was no going back now.

It was 3.22 p.m. and Dad was checking whether the Christmas cakes had cooled yet on their wire trays. The radio was still on and the whole house smelled of sweet spices. I kept listening for news of Santa's Hopefuls but there was nothing. Gramps was watching TV in the front room, while Mum and I started decorating the house with tinsel and garlands of stars.

'Hey! Did you guys hear that?' Dad shouted from the kitchen.

'Hear what?' Mum called back from the stairs where we were looping fairy lights around the banister.

'They've just announced the first Santa Hopeful on the radio,' Dad said. 'A woman called Faith Diaz. She's a world-renowned vet, recently retired. Born in the Philippines but now lives in Singapore with her family.'

'Nice to see a woman get picked first,' Mum commented, sounding pleased.

Excitement zipped through me. The selections had started! Gramps might not have been first, but there were still four more chances.

I spent the rest of the afternoon glued to either the radio or the TV until Dad made me go to the corner shop for some milk. It was a seven-minute walk or a four-minute run. I ran.

At Millie's Mini Mart, I grabbed the milk and joined the back of a long queue. Everyone was talking about the Santa Search. I tapped my foot, desperate to get home.

Ten minutes later, I burst into the kitchen. Mum and Dad were huddled round the radio, listening to it.

'*And we'll be back later to update you on the fourth candidate!*' announced the cheery voice before a Christmas song began to play.

'The *fourth* candidate?' I yelped. 'Who were the second and third?'

'Second was Thomas Reijnders, an award-winning Dutch actor,' said Dad. 'Then there was Becka Moore from New York – I didn't catch her job.'

Only two spots left.

'Where's Gramps?' I asked.

'He's napping,' said Mum. 'Got a bit worn out with all the excitement of the names, I think.'

Just then, the music cut out mid-verse.

'*Coming to you live with more festive news! We have the fourth Hopeful in this once-in-a-lifetime search for a new Santa. Candidate number four is . . . Chad Buckles, millionaire entrepreneur and owner of Buckles Enterprises, from Surrey in England.*'

I bit my lip. Only one spot left.

I spent the next hour refreshing the news page on my tablet. Nothing. I tried to keep calm, remembering something Gran always used to say: hope is the biggest gift of all at Christmas time.

At that moment, a new headline flashed up:

FINAL CANDIDATE IN SANTA SEARCH TO BE ANNOUNCED SHORTLY.

I hurtled downstairs and found Mum and Dad already gathered in front of the TV. I held my breath as the smiling face of a woman with lilac streaks in her hair slowly materialised on-screen.

'Former chef, cat sitter, teacher and pilot, Tara Bakhshi from Australia is the fifth and final candidate!' announced the reporter. 'Congratulations, Tara! Like the other candidates, Tara will be notified where to find her nearest Santa Transport Link so that Santa's Hopefuls can travel to Christmasland together.'

My heart sank.

It was over. All five candidates had been chosen. I glanced at Gramps. He seemed quite content, napping in his armchair. It was just as well I hadn't told him about entering the competition on his behalf.

Despite my huge disappointment that the obvious Santa qualities in Gramps hadn't been recognised, I tried to be cheerful as Mum, Dad

and I finished decorating the tree while Gramps carried on dozing.

One of our favourite Christmas films, *Jingle Jangle*, was playing quietly in the background. I was looking forward to the snowball-fight scene when the film froze and a strange chime rang out from the TV.

The frozen image wobbled and then a newsreader appeared.

She tapped her earpiece, as if she was receiving a piece of important news, then she took a deep breath and said, 'We reported earlier that the fifth and final candidate for Santa Search had been chosen, but we are now hearing rumours that a *sixth* bonus candidate is about to be selected!'

'What a twist!' Dad said. 'That Santa guy is full of surprises.'

DING-DONG!

'Who's that?' Gramps asked, waking up with a snort.

'Oooh, I think that will be some new decorations for the tree,' Mum replied.

'Looks like you're full of surprises as well,' Dad muttered. 'Not sure we needed more decorations, Amma!'

Mum narrowed her eyes at him, and I winced. Dad was certainly feeling brave. He knew better than to get between Mum and her Christmas decorations!

'I'll get it,' I said, and shot out of the living room.

I opened the door and peered up and down the street. There was no one there. It was probably another one of those drop-and-run deliveries. We sometimes had to hunt for packages in case the driver had lobbed them into a bush.

'Down here!'

I looked down and my jaw dropped.

There, on the doorstep, was an elf.

He was dressed in a green suit with a matching

hat, and had a messenger bag slung over one shoulder.

The elf cleared his throat and said, 'Is this the residence of Curtis Merriman?'

I nodded.

'Erm . . . Gramps!' I called into the house. 'You might want to come to the door! There's someone here to see you.'

GRAMPS SHUFFLED INTO THE HALLWAY, rubbing his eyes.

'Curtis Merriman?' the elf asked.

'Yes,' Gramps replied, his forehead creased in confusion.

The elf bent in a deep bow, and the bell at the end of his hat brushed the ground. As he straightened up, he stretched out his hand and a crisp embossed envelope appeared out of thin air.

'I am pleased to inform you that you have been shortlisted for the job of Santa,' said the

elf. 'You are now invited to undergo a series of festive challenges. The finer details are in the letter, along with all the instructions for your nearest Santa Transport Link. Good luck, Curtis Merriman!'

The elf handed the envelope to Gramps and then – *POP!* – he disappeared, vanishing in a burst of glitter.

Gramps stared at the envelope. 'I – I don't understand.'

Curtains along our street were twitching furiously and neighbours ventured outside to see if they really had just seen a Christmas elf disappear in a shimmering cloud of glitter.

'Er . . . I should explain,' I said, shutting the door.

Over the sound of my pounding heartbeat, I heard Gramps's name being announced on the TV.

'*In a surprise twist of events, Curtis Merriman from Liverpool, England, retired bus driver, is the*

sixth and final candidate to be selected as a Santa Hopeful in this dramatic end to a thrilling day!'

'What's going on, Mikey?' asked Gramps.

'Um . . . I kind of submitted an application for you,' I began. 'I know you don't feel very Christmassy right now, Gramps, but I really believe that meeting Santa might help you love Christmas again. And you did say Christmas is going to be different without Gran,' I added softly, 'so why not try something completely different?'

'Mikey!' said Mum and Dad, joining us in the hallway. 'You should have asked Gramps first!'

Gramps rubbed his face wearily, different emotions flickering across it like candlelight. I could almost see the old happy memories from past Christmases with Gran going through his mind.

'Is that what all those questions earlier were about?' asked Gramps.

I nodded my head sheepishly.

'Oh, Mikey Boy! I'm not the right person for the job,' he said with a sigh.

But I didn't hear an outright *no*.

'You're allowed to take someone with you to help with the challenges,' I said, nudging his arm as I made my best please-take-me-with-you-to-meet-Santa face.

A tiny smile played on Gramps's lips, like the beginning of a sunrise.

'Pleeeeease,' I begged.

'I suppose it means I won't have to face the community centre grotto without Claudette this year,' Gramps said, almost to himself. 'And if I'm going to do this, I can't think of anyone better I'd like to take as a plus-one!'

'Yesss!' I cried, punching the air.

'We'll have to get in touch with school,' Mum said. 'Tell them you won't be in.' She wrinkled her nose. 'We don't even know how long you'll be gone for . . .'

'Mikey's head teacher loves Christmas almost as much as us – I think it'll be fine,' said Dad. 'Besides, this will be an education like no other!'

'We're not going to win though,' said Gramps, looking at us. 'You know that, right? I don't want you all getting your hopes up.'

I just grinned.

Gramps let out a deep sigh, but then smiled and passed the envelope to me. 'OK, Mikey. Do the honours and tell us what the letter says.'

I tore it open while Gramps, Mum and Dad peered over my shoulders.

**The Santa Transport Link for
Curtis Merriman will be at the Big Wheel
at Liverpool Christmas Market.**

**Be there by 7 p.m. today or face
IMMEDIATE disqualification.**

'But that's only twenty minutes away!' Mum exclaimed.

'You'll never make it,' said Dad, wringing his hands. 'The car's at the garage being fixed!'

POOF! A glowing timer appeared on the letter, counting down the minutes to seven o'clock. I was amazed by the magic for all of one second, then I remembered there was no time to lose!

Clutching the letter, I raced to my room and emptied out my school backpack, scattering textbooks everywhere. I frantically started packing: a notebook, pens, clothes, toothbrush, toothpaste and a small tub of curl cream, because Mum says you should never leave your hair thirsty.

'I can't get a taxi!' Mum called upstairs. 'No one is accepting bookings.'

'Maybe someone could give us a lift?' I cried from the landing, glancing at the timer on the letter. Ten minutes to go.

Wearing his green woollen coat and flat cap, Gramps was waiting for me by the front door with his bag as I raced down the stairs. He slipped on his thick black boots. I quickly flung on a padded jacket and laced up my oldest, comfiest trainers before darting into the living room to pop the Gran-Angel from the top of the tree into my bag. It was my way of bringing Gran with us – Mum

was so touched that she didn't even tell me off for walking inside the house with my shoes on.

'Right. Are you ready, Gramps?' I said, hauling my bag over my shoulder.

Gramps nodded, looking excited and queasy as I opened the front door.

I gasped. It seemed as if everyone in Toxteth was gathered outside!

'Woohoo! Curtis for Santa!'

'Will you sign my apron?'

'If you get the job, don't forget to put me on the Nice List!'

'Can someone give us a lift to the Big Wheel? We need to be there by seven!' I yelled over the noise.

Bob from over the road pushed his way through the crowd. 'Get in the van! I'll get you there on time.'

'You legend,' said Gramps.

'It's nothing,' Bob replied, leading me and

Gramps to his vehicle. 'You and Claudette were so kind to me when I was ill a couple of years ago. Honestly, I don't know what I'd have done without your stews and that Saturday soup!'

Bob slid the van door open and ushered us to sit next to him in the front seats.

'Good luck! We love you!' Mum and Dad shouted, their voices tiny over the din of the crowds. 'Send us messages and let us know how you're getting on!'

Bob revved the engine and switched his headlights on. The whole street cheered.

'Hold on tight and belt up! I'll get you there on time if my name isn't Bob Cratchit.'

The van lurched forward and then sped down the road. Gramps held on to his cap as I waved at the excited crowd.

Six minutes left and counting . . .

6

BOB DROVE FURIOUSLY FAST. I HAD NO IDEA a rusty old van could go at such speed.

I grabbed Gramps's arm as Bob zoomed round another corner and down an empty street.

'Bob, please slow down!' said Gramps. 'I think I hear sirens!'

I glanced in the side mirrors. A police car was gaining on us, flashing its lights.

'We need to pull over!' I yelled.

'I'll pull over, all right,' said Bob, slamming

his foot down on the accelerator. 'Just as soon as we get you to that Big Wheel!'

I watched Bob lean forward in his seat, gripping the steering wheel as he stared at the road. Was he enjoying this?!

The timer on the letter was counting down the last minute. We were never going to make it!

'Argh!' I cried as Bob screeched round another corner, shouting, 'Hold on!'

The van tipped to the side on two wheels . . . before bumping back down, right in front of the Big Wheel. Thirty seconds to go.

Gramps and I scrambled out of the van but then froze in shocked awe.

'Santa's turned the Big Wheel into a giant snowflake,' I whispered.

It was gleaming white and made entirely out of snow and ice. Between the arms of a six-pointed snowflake were carriages carved out of ice.

'They're here!' a girl with dark hair cried from

above as Gramps and I scrambled into the last empty snowflake carriage. She was leaning out of the carriage's hexagonal window and spoke with a twang I could not quite place.

Gramps and I high-fived. My heart was pounding. We'd made it!

'Excuse me, but who's in charge here?' came a man's rather posh voice from one of the other carriages. 'It's been rather tiresome criss-crossing the world collecting people in this Santa Link contraption. And I think these two were late.'

'Oh, come on. Have a little Christmas spirit, will you?' called a woman with an Australian accent and lilac streaks in her hair from another carriage. 'They made it just in time.' I recognised her face from the announcement about Tara Bakhshi. Contestant number five.

The Big Wheel started turning as soon as we closed the door.

Bob was jumping up and down with excitement, waving us off. 'Say hi to Santa from me!'

The police car screeched to a stop next to Bob, and a police officer stormed out, looking furious. Bob said something and pointed at the Big Wheel. The police officer peered upwards, shielding her eyes from the glare of the icy, glittering structure. I saw her jaw drop.

'Tell Santa thank you for the doll house I got when I was seven. Best present EVER!' she yelled.

Our snowflake carriage stopped at the very top, where all of Liverpool was spread below us like a carpet of twinkling lights. I got to my feet and gazed around.

'Hey, Gramps. I think the other Hopefuls have ALL brought kids with them too!' I said.

'Makes sense, Mikey. Kids help make Christm—' Gramps broke off.

CREAAAK.

I froze.

'Did you hear that?' Gramps asked, his eyes wide now.

'Err . . .' I peered outside. My throat went dry. A bolt. A really chunky one had come loose where our snowflake carriage was joined to the rest of the Big Wheel.

Below us, the other Hopefuls and their helpers were standing up and pointing at our carriage. The whole structure swayed.

CREAAAAAK.

The bolt jolted again. Just a tiny bit. But enough.

'Everyone, stop moving!' I shouted as loud as I could while standing absolutely still. 'This bolt is going to come off – you're making it worse!'

Everyone went still and silent. Dead still. Dead silent. Even the wind seemed to hush.

I stared at the bolt. It shifted again . . . then seemed to slip back into place.

Gramps let out a ragged breath.

'It just needed a moment,' he said.

I didn't say anything. I sat down slowly, eyes still on that bolt.

'How long are we going to be here?' a woman with an American accent asked loudly. 'There's no Santa, is there? This is all some kind of trick!'

'It's not a trick,' shouted a kid with big glasses, from another carriage. I think he had a Dutch accent because he sounded a tiny bit like my favourite football player, Virgil Van Dijk. 'Look up there!'

Whoa.

Electric shades of swirling green, yellow, purple and blue had bloomed in one corner of the sky. It was exactly like what we'd learned about at school. The Northern Lights!

'Cooyah,' Gramps breathed. 'The aurora borealis . . . here in Liverpool!'

The whirling colours began to pull apart from

each other, revealing a deep blue core at their centre. I rubbed my eyes. Was there something moving inside?

'Are those what I think they are?' whispered Gramps.

We all went silent as the sound of jingling bells rang over the Big Wheel.

Eight majestic reindeer burst out of the swirl of colour, pulling a red-and-gold sleigh and an elf who held the reins.

'Now, Dasher! Now, Dancer! Now, Prancer and Vixen!' cried the elf. 'On Comet! On Cupid! On Donder and Blitzen!'

I shivered with excitement.

'This is actually, really happening,' I murmured. I didn't dare blink. I didn't want to miss any of this.

The reindeer gracefully arced across the moonlit sky and slowed to a halt, hovering next to us by the Big Wheel.

The elf got to his feet. 'I am Chief Elf, please

listen carefully.' He picked up a scroll from the seat next to him, then unfurled it with a flourish. He stuck his nose in the air and cleared his throat.

'Faith Diaz,

Thomas Reijnders,

Becka Moore,

Chad Buckles,

Tara Bakhshi

and Curtis Merriman . . .

Congratulations! You have been shortlisted to compete for the prestigious role of Santa and will take part in a series of challenges. Now, please stay seated while your carriages are secured to the sleigh, ready for our journey to Christmasland.'

The elf fiddled with something on his dashboard, and an icy chain shot out of the back of the sleigh, attaching itself firmly to the nearest snowflake carriage. *CLICK!* Satisfied, the elf expertly steered the reindeer round the

Big Wheel, linking carriages to each other like a train.

'A sleigh ride to Christmasland, Mikey!' exclaimed Gramps, as excited chatter broke out all around us. 'We could go home right this minute and I'd have stories for the rest of my days!'

'Hold on, Gramps. We haven't even met Santa yet!' I grinned. 'And then you've got to win the—' I broke off as our carriage gave a huge jolt.

SCREEEEECH.

The bolt! The chunky one that had been wobbling. It was gone! Just . . . *gone.*

Gramps and I gasped as the carriage gave another violent judder. My stomach twisted as I realised something.

We weren't attached to the Big Wheel any more!

'Help!' Gramps and I cried, grabbing the sides as the carriage tilted.

I caught a glimpse of Chief Elf, who was only metres away, his eyes wide.

And then our snowflake carriage . . .

fell.

7

'**A**AAAARGH!' I SCREAMED, AND GRAMPS hugged me close.

My eyes squeezed tight, I heard the grunt of reindeer, followed by the sound of swishing, sizzling magic . . . Then, all of a sudden, we jolted to a stop.

'Oof!' Gramps groaned as we slammed back in our seats.

I opened my eyes. Our carriage was suspended in mid-air, just above the ground. I peered over the side. The elf had attached our carriage to the chain at the very last second.

'Blouse and skirt!' exclaimed Gramps, who had miraculously managed to keep his cap on his head. 'That was close.'

'You're telling me,' I muttered.

Chief Elf's face appeared at our window, one elbow casually resting on the edge of the sleigh. 'I did tell you to stay seated. Now, reindeer, dash away!'

WHOOSH! The sleigh shot upwards, taking all six snowflake carriages with it like a magic roller coaster. We were flying!

The reindeer soared over Liverpool, bells jingling, while tiny figures below pointed up in amazement. I waved frantically when we passed Toxteth, even though I was sure Mum and Dad couldn't see us. I was going to miss them.

We climbed higher towards the Northern Lights. My ears popped as we rocketed directly into the heart of the swirling colours.

Then came a crackle from a hidden speaker in our carriage.

'*Please remain seated,*' Chief Elf announced, sounding exactly like a pilot. '*We expect turbulence.*'

I stuck my arm outside as we drove through, the colours flowing in between my fingers. I looked at Gramps and he had the biggest smile I'd seen in ages. He'd reached out his hand as well, magical light flowing over his palm.

This was going to work! I was going to get my old Gramps back!

There was a tinkling of bells as we burst out of the swirling tunnel of colours and found ourselves in a wide, dark sky glittering with stars. Beneath us were little wooden cabins nestled upon bright white snow. We flew past a grand wooden sign that read:

WELCOME TO CHRISTMASLAND

It was a lot different from what we'd seen on TV, and by 'different' I mean a zillion times better, with never-ending snowy hills and tree-lined glades glowing in the moonlight. The cabin roofs looked like they'd been topped with the fluffiest whipped cream.

We dipped lower, sweeping past giant fir trees that smelled of winter pine, and then the sleigh glided down into a cosy Christmas village where chimney smoke curled through the cold air.

'This is it, Gramps,' I whispered.

'This is it, Mikey Boy,' he whispered back.

We climbed out of our carriage, legs wobbly, sinking into the softest snow. The other Hopefuls looked just as amazed as we all stared around. I glanced at the Helpers – they all seemed to be a similar age to me. I wondered if that was just a coincidence.

'Welcome to Christmasland!' announced Chief Elf, hopping down from the sleigh. 'Secret heart

of the North Pole. As mentioned previously, I'm Chief Elf – but what I didn't tell you is that I am also the Head of Santa Search and Other Top-Secret Yuletide Operations.'

'Wait! Wait for me to do the intros!' came a high-pitched voice. A fairy emerged from a nearby cabin, her dress glittering like tinsel. She looked younger than Chief Elf.

Chief Elf folded his arms and sighed.

'I want to say the biggest and warmest welcome from all of us here at Christmasland,' the fairy said, breathless but smiling at each of us in turn.

'The humans have already been welcomed, Sugar Plum,' grumbled Chief Elf.

'I'm Deputy Head of Santa Search and Other

Top-Secret Yuletide Operations,' she said, ignoring him. 'Can't wait to get to know everyone. I watched all your videos many times over.'

'Are you – are you a fairy?' gasped the Dutch boy.

Sugar Plum laughed and fluttered her wings. 'Why, yes, Bram Reijnders! I'm a rare Sugar Plum Fairy-Elf. That's why I'm called . . . er . . . Sugar Plum. We're really original when it comes to names in this place,' she added with a wink, then she giggled and it sounded like the cheeriest of festive bells.

'Actually, I don't think we got your name, Mr Chief Elf,' Gramps asked.

'Chief Elf will do just fine,' the elf replied.

'Charming,' Gramps said under his breath.

'When do we meet Santa?' called a bored-sounding voice from behind us. It was a boy with sandy-coloured hair. 'Not someone's uncle in a red costume and a padded suit. I mean, the *real* one.'

'Tomorrow morning,' said Chief Elf, clapping his hands. 'Now it's time for sleep. Hopefuls, follow Sugar Plum. Helpers, come with me. Oh, and before I forget – we've let your families know that you've arrived safely. You can send them a Santa Mail tomorrow if you like, or try your phones but the signal doesn't work well here. The satellites struggle with cutting through Christmas magic.'

Gramps turned to me and smiled. 'What a journey already. I can't wait to see what's next.'

'Me neither,' I said.

He pulled me into one of his big, warm hugs.

'Goodnight, Mikey.'

'Goodnight, Gramps.'

Chief Elf was already halfway up a path, snow flying from his boots. I dashed after him through the dark. We stopped outside a two-storey, biscuit-coloured lodge. The windows glowed with amber warmth and a chimney wrapped with

liquorice-like laces puffed gentle smoke into the sky.

'Ginger,' sniffed a girl with a bouncy ponytail and Australian accent. 'And . . . cinnamon?' She ran to the window and broke off a bit of the ledge. 'I knew it! Gingerbread!'

'Mina Bakhshi!' barked Chief Elf, snatching the piece of ledge from her. 'Please do not eat the house.'

He tried to stick it back on, but it dropped into the snow.

I squinted. The walls weren't wood. They were biscuit! And the roof wasn't covered in snow but *cream icing*.

'Er . . . are we really staying in a gingerbread house?' I asked.

'I knew that chimney looked weird. Those laces are liquorice!' said a girl with shoulder-length dark hair. She grinned at me. 'I'm Ella Diaz, by the way.'

'Mikey Merriman,' I said, grinning back.

'This isn't some Hansel and Gretel thing, is it?' asked the boy with sandy hair and a posh English accent. His arms were crossed. 'What if a witch comes and gobbles us up in the night?'

Mina dropped the peppermint swirl she'd peeled off the wall in horror.

Another girl with curly dark hair in bunches gasped.

'That's just a fairy tale,' said Ella.

'So was Santa Claus,' said the boy. 'And yet . . . here we are.'

Bram Reijnders gulped and looked queasy. I felt bad for him. It's not fun to be worried about getting eaten by a witch.

'I am happy to arrange a sleigh ride home if you would rather stay somewhere else, Jackson Buckles,' said Chief Elf, tapping his foot impatiently. 'Now, those who wish to stay in Christmasland . . . follow me!'

Jackson gave the exterior of the house a thoughtful look, then followed Chief Elf inside. The rest of us went after him.

Chief Elf swiftly gave us a very serious tour of the house, with warnings not to nibble any of the marshmallow sofas or other edible furniture items. He showed us a rainbow-swirled bell to ring if there was an emergency and then took us up the candy-cane stairs to a huge room. Six cosy beds were arranged on different levels. One bed was tucked into a loft space bordered with wafer railings, while another bed was snuggled under a slanting honeycomb beam. Each bed had fluffy red pyjamas folded neatly at the foot, which were wrapped with gold ribbons. A fire crackled in welcome at the other end of the room.

I claimed the bed next to a jelly-bean-edged window and sat on it.

'I will leave you now to get ready for bed – it's been a long day,' said Chief Elf, softening

slightly. 'A proper breakfast will be waiting downstairs in the morning. Get a good night's sleep as you will be meeting Santa tomorrow and taking part in the first challenge. Let's just say it will be . . . thrilling.' With that, he shut the door with a quiet click.

Ella's voice drifted down from her wafer-railed bed. 'If this is a dream, I don't want to wake up!'

8

I WOKE UP TO THE SMELL OF GINGERBREAD, icing sugar and jelly beans.

I opened my eyes and grinned. My bedroom at home didn't have honeycomb beams or gumdrops stuck on the walls. It hadn't been a dream. Gramps and I really were in Christmasland!

Yesterday, as soon as we were sure that Chief Elf had gone, me and the rest of the kids had all crept out of bed and tiptoed downstairs to explore. The living-room curtains tasted like strawberry laces. And the plates in the kitchen?

They were sherbet flying saucers!

That's when I properly met the others.

Ella lived in Singapore with her parents and her gran, who she called Lola. I thought that was her gran's name at first, which confused me because Dad had said she was called Faith, but Ella explained that 'lola' was Filipino for 'grandmother', and 'lolo' was 'grandfather'.

The girl with curly hair in bunches was Sophia. At home in America, she rode horses – 'proper jumps and everything'. She said that if her Auntie Becka won, she was going to quit school to help her auntie out as Santa full-time.

Mina was the one who tried to eat the door frame. She was from Australia.

Bram, who had been worried about getting eaten by a witch, didn't want to eat any sweets because he had already brushed his teeth.

And Jackson? Well, he spent the whole time calculating how much the gingerbread lodge

would cost to build in a factory. He was sure there would be a market for it.

Once we'd had our fill of curtains and crockery, we snuck back upstairs and into bed. (But only after Bram had made sure that we all brushed our teeth!)

As I'd lain under the covers, everything else that had happened earlier that day came rushing back to me like a glorious Christmas movie (apart from the almost-falling-to-our-doom bit, of course). We'd taken a magical sleigh ride through the Northern Lights to Christmasland! And we were going to meet Santa in the morning, to do our first Santa Search challenge.

Now that we were here, I really wanted Gramps to win, more than anything. I'd drifted off to sleep thinking about how brilliant it would be to see Gramps as Father Christmas, riding a sleigh pulled by magic reindeer.

Taking in the amazing smell of gingerbread,

I blinked and rubbed my eyes. I sat up and looked around the massive bedroom. All the other beds were empty – *they must be at breakfast!* I got ready and raced down to the kitchen.

Chief Elf hadn't been joking. A 'proper' breakfast stretched across the table like something out of a dream – buttermilk pancakes, sugar-dusted French toast, cranberry scones, and gooey eggs on muffins . . . There were also bowls of cinnamon-spiced oatmeal, fresh rolls, ham, cheeses, and even chocolate croissants stacked high like treasure.

'You've got to try these pancakes, Mikey,' said Ella, maple syrup glistening on her chin.

'I might need two plates,' I said, eyeing the feast.

'French toast is even better,' said Mina, licking icing sugar from her fingertips.

'You'll rot your teeth,' Bram muttered, frowning over his milk.

'No drama. That's what baby teeth are for,' Mina replied, taking a huge bite of French toast.

I sat next to Jackson, who was dressed in a red tracksuit with 'SANTA IN TRAINING' down the leg. He was glued to his phone. My parents wouldn't let me have one yet.

'Morning,' I said.

'Shh,' he hissed. 'I'm in the middle of a deal.'

'He hasn't said a word to us,' Mina stage-whispered, 'but every time the phone rings he yells, "Jackson Buckles speaking!" like he's on *The Apprentice*.'

'Business does not stop for Christmas,' Jackson announced. 'I've almost secured exclusive tuck-shop rights at school, but my reception keeps on cutting out.'

'That will be the Christmas magic, interfering with the phone signal,' Bram said with a disapproving expression. 'Besides, at the table, phones aren't allowed.'

'Rules, shmules – who's gonna stop us? There're no grown-ups around,' said Sophia, piling more food onto her plate.

I felt a stab of guilt at that. There were definitely *some* rules I hadn't followed when I'd entered Gramps into the competition without telling him. But Gramps didn't know that.

The others started chatting about what the first challenge might be.

'If they've got reindeer rides, I'm totally first in line!' Sophia declared.

'And I'll be right behind you!' chimed Ella.

I wasn't so sure I'd be as eager as them for a reindeer ride. The last animal I rode was a donkey when I was on holiday, and that hadn't gone too well.

'Water, anyone?' Ella asked, heading for the sink. She froze as she turned the tap handle. 'No. Way.'

She leaned over and drank straight from the

spout. When she looked up, her face was smeared with . . .

'Hot chocolate!' she cried. 'It's actual hot chocolate on tap!'

Mina and Sophia bolted for the sink, and I followed. (Jackson was still on his phone.) The drink was silky smooth, spiced just right, with a hint of salted caramel, and not too hot.

'But, guys, this cannot be hygienic,' Bram protested.

'It's Christmasland,' said Mina. 'Chocolate taps are totally allowed.'

Before Bram could argue, a loudspeaker boomed through the house.

'*Calling all Santa's Hopefuls and Helpers to the village square! Your first Santa Search challenge awaits!*'

We scrambled to get ready. A coat stand had

appeared overnight, piled with jackets, scarves, mittens and hats in every colour.

I pulled on silver snow boots, a blue bomber jacket, red gloves and a furry hat.

Outside, we followed the signs through the snow to the village square.

'There's Gramps!' I waved to him. He was still in his old woollen coat and green flat cap.

'And that's my lola next to him!' Ella said, grinning.

Ella's grandmother was wearing a huge coat with a snowflake pattern running across her hat and scarf. She waited until Gramps and I had hugged before shaking my hand warmly.

'It's lovely to meet you, Mikey,' she said. 'Call me Lola Faith. Your lolo has been telling me all about you.'

We joined the other Hopefuls in front of a small stage and I realised it was the same stand where Santa had made his retirement announcement.

In the morning light, Christmasland looked like a scene straight out of a Christmas card. I didn't have a way to take a photo, so I squeezed my eyes shut, hoping it would stick in my memory instead.

'At least we're not the last to arrive this time,' said Gramps. 'Santa's still not here.'

Lola Faith shuddered. 'Can you imagine how organised he has to be to do this job and get presents to everyone? I don't think I could ever be *that* organised.'

'Not true, Lola – look how quickly we got the application sent off,' Ella reminded her. 'We were pretty organised then!'

'True, iha,' Lola Faith said.

'You were the first candidate to be announced, weren't you?' I asked.

'Yep!' Ella nodded. 'I'm so glad we were the first because we got to see where everyone else lived. Our Santa Transport Link was the Singapore

Flyer – it was amazing to see it looking like a huge snowflake, especially since it never snows in Singapore. We got taken to the Netherlands to pick up Bram and Thomas, then went on to New York for Sophia and Becka. After that, we—'

POP!

Chief Elf appeared on stage in a cloud of glitter. He unrolled a sheet of paper and tapped a small, elf-sized microphone next to the main stand.

'Please step forward when you hear your names,' he announced. 'Faith and Ella Diaz . . . Thomas and Bram Reijnders . . . Becka and Sophia Moore . . . Chad and Jackson Buckles . . . Tara and Mina Bakhshi . . . Curtis and Mikey Merriman.'

In pairs, we stepped forward to the edge of the stage, and an elf swiftly took our picture.

'For the journalists,' the elf explained. 'Everyone is very excited to see how you are getting on.'

| MIKEY MERRIMAN | CURTIS MERRIMAN |

| FAITH DIAZ | ELLA DIAZ |

| SOPHIA MOORE | BECKA MOORE |

| CHAD BUCKLES | JACKSON BUCKLES |

| THOMAS REIJNDERS | BRAM REIJNDERS |

| MINA BAKHSHI | TARA BAKHSHI |

'You will now receive a contract that *must* be signed before you can take part in the Santa Search challenges,' Chief Elf said, impatiently shooing the camera-elf away. He clicked his fingers. *POP!* A stack of papers appeared, which he handed to all the grown-ups.

Gramps peered at the contract over his glasses, holding it close to his face. 'Mikey, it's no good. My glasses are only for long distance and this writing is tiny. You'll have to read this and let me know what it says.'

I took the contract from Gramps, my stomach twisting as I read it. On the third line, the contract stated that all rules need to have been followed when applying to Santa Search. But I hadn't followed them. The video hadn't been recent, and Gramps hadn't entered himself.

'I'm sure it's fine to sign,' Gramps said, searching his pockets for a pen. 'And remember, Mikey: I'm not here to win. We'll meet Santa,

hear the first task, and if it's not for us, we'll go home, OK?'

I didn't say anything. But I knew for sure that Gramps did not deserve to go home. It already felt like ages since I'd submitted his application. We'd come so far. So, yes, I'd bent the rules a little but hadn't broken them completely . . . had I?

Had I?

I bit my lip, ready to confess when actual, real-life Santa swept into the village square in a huge red-and-gold sleigh, his reindeer trotting through the soft piles of Christmasland snow. *Whoa!*

Gramps took the contract out of my hand and signed it before I could speak.

9

A MURMUR OF EXCITEMENT RIPPLED through the Hopefuls and the Helpers. Santa looked exactly like he did on TV but seeing him here in Christmasland made my breath catch in my throat. Gramps seemed even more amazed than I was.

'Cooyah . . . this is really something,' Gramps said. 'If only . . .'

He didn't finish, but I knew he was thinking of Gran. I'd been thinking about her a lot too. Something about this place made it easy to forget that she wasn't still here and then the memory of her being gone would creep up on you.

Chief Elf raised a hand for quiet, and Santa stepped down from his sleigh and walked to the stage. Gramps's hand trembled on my shoulder.

'Ho ho ho and merry Christmas!' Santa boomed. 'Welcome, welcome, everyone! Christmasland will be your home for the next couple of days. But for one of you, it may become home for much longer. Each of you was chosen because I saw something in you. A quality that could ensure the future of Christmas, be it kindness, determination or creativity, but only one can become the next Santa. Today you all stand equal in possibility and I wish you the best of luck.'

Gramps gave my shoulder a squeeze.

'The first task begins shortly,' Santa continued. 'There will be four challenges in total – each one drawn from my own experiences and designed

by Chief Elf. You will be awarded points in these tasks: six points for first place, five points for second place, four points for third place, and so on. At the end of the third challenge, Hopefuls with the lowest score will be sent home, leaving just three candidates remaining. Your performance will help me decide who should be the winner of this competition. Are there any questions?'

'Chad Buckles here. Not a question, just a statement of appreciation,' he said smoothly. 'My son, Jackson, and I are honoured to be here, and especially excited to work with Chief Elf. We couldn't ask for a better guide.'

Jackson beamed. 'We're huge fans of Chief Elf. And are very aware that he is always on hand to remind you of all and any of the six hundred and seventy-three rules in the Christmasland manual. Including Rule 399: *If a mince pie is left out past its prime, Santa may regift it to a creature of wing or foot.*'

Ella frowned. 'How do they know all this?' she hissed.

I shrugged. I had no idea.

Santa chuckled. 'Ah, yes, there really are a lot of rules. Impressive knowledge of the mince-pie protocol, by the way.'

'We've done our research,' Chad replied modestly.

Sugar Plum fluttered onto the stage. She seemed a bit irritated. Maybe it was all the Chief Elf praise from the Buckles. 'Let's begin, shall we? Time for your first task, which *I* very much enjoyed designing.'

Gramps leaned in. 'Remember, Mikey, it's been such an adventure to even come to Christmasland. That's enough in itself. We're not going to win this competition, you know that, right? Look at the Buckles. They're born for this.'

I crossed my arms. 'Gran always said there's no such thing as *can't*.'

Gramps smiled. 'Yes, that was one of her favourites. She was the most stubborn person I'd ever met.' He blew out a breath. 'OK, let's hear the first task and see if we fancy it.'

Sugar Plum tapped the mic. 'Good morning, Hopefuls and Helpers! Your first challenge is *navigation*. Each team will use a magical map to find the Candy Cane of Destiny. There you must retrieve a wooden reindeer ornament, to prove that you reached your destination. You'll each be given one of our smaller, two-reindeer sleighs for transport. First team to return wins, and this will decide the leader board.'

Chatter broke out among everyone. I turned to Gramps, and he gave me a thumbs up. Looks like we were doing the first task! I wasn't surprised, though. Gramps used to be a bus driver before he retired. He'd driven in both London and Liverpool. I bet he couldn't wait to ride own sleigh.

We all followed Chief Elf and Sugar Plum to the stables, where peppermint-scented hay and reindeer breath filled the cold air. Sugar Plum took me and Gramps to meet our reindeer for the challenge – Aurora and Tempest.

'I'd give them some sugar snap peas before climbing into the sleigh,' Sugar Plum suggested, handing over some pea pods. 'Christmas reindeer have quite the sweet tooth, but they need to avoid *too* much sugar. It can make them sleepy if they get a sugar crash.'

Our reindeer loved the treat and chomped on the pods eagerly.

Sugar Plum smiled at us. 'It's lovely to meet both of you properly. I loved your application, by the way.' She shook her head. 'Can you believe it ended up in the spam folder? Our filters were set to block bogus entries, but clearly got a bit too enthusiastic. We only found the video at the last minute and Santa was adamant that you were

added. That's why you were such a late addition.'

'Really?' Gramps replied. ' I didn't ev—'

'I wonder if we should get in the sleigh,' I cut in. Gramps did *not* need to hear any more about the application process. 'We're about to start.'

'Choose who will be navigating, please!' Chief Elf yelled.

After some discussion, we decided that it should be me because Gramps didn't have his reading glasses . . . then *POP!* A magical map appeared in my hands. It was like no map I'd seen before. The ink kept shifting as if the map was alive. Was it supposed to do that?

We gave our reindeer a pat on the head, then climbed into the sleigh. Eagerly, Gramps picked up the reindeer reins.

'Remember, this is a test of teamwork, paying attention and getting to your destination in good time,' Sugar Plum said. 'Misread your map and

you could end up in Yule-Be-Sorry Canyon. Guide your sleigh incorrectly and you might end up in the Forest of Bad Tidings.'

'A bit of help here?' Chad called out. He and Jackson had their arms tangled in the reins.

I turned to Gramps. 'See? Even the Buckles don't get everything right.'

Sugar Plum helped the Buckles untangle themselves as she ran through a few things: how to hold the reins, how to stay calm. 'Reindeer pick up on your nerves,' she warned.

'Find the Candy Cane of Destiny, find your wooden reindeer. First sleigh back will go to the top of the leader board!' Chief Elf called. 'Get ready . . . set . . . go, go, go!'

Gramps whooped as we took off into the sky.

I clutched the map, reading it carefully as we flew over Cedar Lake and Mistletoe Valley. The ink had stopped shifting about, which was good. We passed the glowing outline of Chocolate

Molten Mountains, and Gramps looked like he was in his element. Steady hands, sure turns, totally relaxed. Like he was back driving the Number 82A bus.

I glanced at the map and saw that each Hopeful was represented by a small golden dot with their name below it. We were in third place. Ella and Lola Faith were in the lead, with the Buckles a close second. The Reijnders were bobbing behind us with the Bakhshis. The Moores had started slow but were gaining fast.

'Gramps? Can we push it a bit? We're about to drop into fourth.'

He wrinkled his nose. 'A galloping horse can't hear the sound of his own backfoot.'

'Huh?' I said. Gran had loved a proverb; she always said proverbs were advice wrapped in love. Gramps didn't use them so often, but today was different, clearly!

Gramps chuckled. 'I mean, rushing leads to

mistakes, Mikey. Besides, Aurora and Tempest know what they're doing and still have loads left in the tank. They'll know the right moment to shift gear.'

WHOOSH!

The Moores zipped past, barely looking back.

I bit my tongue. Gramps wasn't worried, but I was.

We sailed over Myrrh Brook, only to plunge into fog so thick I couldn't even make out the tips of our reindeer's antlers.

'Can't see a thing,' Gramps muttered. 'Let's try the headlights.'

He pressed a button and thin beams cut through the mist, but it wasn't nearly enough. Everything beyond the reindeer blurred into swirling greys and whites. I peered at the map, squinting as the magical ink started shifting around again, blinking in and out of visibility.

'Right,' I cried. 'No, wait . . . Left! No, right!'

The sleigh jolted hard, as we changed direction but Gramps kept his grip steady. His expression was intense. There was a spark in him I hadn't seen in a while. Like someone had lit a fire inside of him.

'Mikey, I think I see the Candy Cane of Destiny. Just ahead. Check the map.'

I peered down. He was right. Aurora and Tempest must have found a shortcut through Mistletoe Valley, because the Candy Cane of Destiny was really close when it had seemed so far away only minutes ago.

'Gramps!' I cried. 'You were right! The reindeer did know best!'

Aurora and Tempest snorted in agreement.

We burst out of the fog and into dazzling winter sunlight. The sky stretched bright and endless above us, and the snow below gleamed as if it had been sprinkled with crushed diamonds. And there it was.

The Candy Cane of Destiny rose out of the ground. It was much bigger than a regular candy cane – I reckon it was twice the height of Gramps!

'Yes! Gramps, go!' I shouted, leaning over the edge of the sleigh.

Suddenly the map in my hands gave a soft

crackle. The ink shimmered, then flickered again. The tiny glowing dots that represented each team were still moving – except one.

'Gramps . . . Hang on.'

Ella and Lola Faith's dot, which had been leading before we entered the fog, had fallen far behind. Really far behind.

I tapped their dot. The map responded, zooming in until I could see the faint outline of rocky terrain below the glowing marker. Oh no! It looked like they were on the edge of the Ice Cliffs. The dot wasn't moving, but it started to flash amber and then red, blinking rapidly.

Ella and Lola Faith weren't just off-track. They were in real trouble.

10

'**IT'S ELLA AND LOLA FAITH – I THINK THEY'RE**
stuck on a cliff,' I explained to Gramps. 'They're
in danger!'

'Take me to them,' Gramps said, his voice calm
but determined.

I pointed in the direction of the fog and, with a
flick of the reins, Gramps steered the sleigh round
and galloped straight back into dense mist.

As Aurora and Tempest charged ahead,
I realised we were throwing away our chance
of reaching the Candy Cane of Destiny, and the

wooden reindeer that waited there, but I didn't care. We needed to make sure our new friends were safe.

'I can't see through all this fog, Mikey,' Gramps murmured, slowing down once we reached the Ice Cliffs. 'We'll need to go slowly and I'm going to need you to be my eyes and ears, OK?'

'Always, Gramps,' I said.

We navigated our way through a ravine, with the terrifying Ice Cliffs looming on either side. Jagged, black ice jutted out in all directions, like a hundred waves had frozen mid-crash. The whistling wind rocked the sleigh fiercely. Beneath us, the deep, dark drop seemed to go on forever.

Without warning, a pillar of ice appeared out of the gloom.

'Gramps!' I shouted, tugging at his sleeve.

He yanked the reins, and the sleigh lurched sideways, narrowly missing the pillar.

Cautiously, we dipped and veered between

frozen towers of stone and ice. I could hear my ragged breath in my ears, even over the wind. Aurora and Tempest started to neigh anxiously.

'Steady, Mikey,' Gramps said. 'Remember what Sugar Plum told us? The reindeer pick up on what we're feeling. If we stay calm, they will too.'

I nodded, taking in deep, slow breaths. Then I saw it – a flash of red. Ella and Lola Faith's sleigh. I directed Gramps and, as we got closer, I saw that Ella and her grandma were stuck on a snow-covered outcrop, their sleigh balanced dangerously close to the edge, with a single rock stopping them from sliding into the dark below. Their reindeer were nowhere in sight.

'I don't know if we can get down there,' Gramps said. 'The wind is too fierce.'

'So what do we do?' I asked.

Gramps looked worried. 'We need a different route to them.'

Aurora and Tempest gave a whinny and a second later they were galloping onwards, curving round a sharp bend in the ravine.

'No! We can't leave them,' I cried.

But Gramps touched my shoulder. 'I think Aurora and Tempest have a plan. Trust them, Mikey.'

The reindeer landed on a wide shelf of rock, facing the wall of ice. With a jingle of bells, the sleigh surged forward. *CRACK!* The reindeer hit the ice with their massive antlers.

'Aaaargh!' Gramps and I yelled, clutching each other as shards of ice splintered off in every direction.

The sleigh surged forward again, and then – *SMASH!*

I gasped. The reindeer were smashing their way into the cliff! They kept on going until they'd smashed a passageway all the way through to the other side.

'Well done, Tempest! Well done, Aurora!' Gramps exclaimed.

We came out of the cliff just above Ella and her lola. The wind was still howling. One jolt or judder and they could fall.

Gramps adjusted our angle in the air. 'Mikey, take the reins. I'll need to pull them in. Fast.'

'It's going to take both of us,' I said firmly.

Gramps paused, but then nodded. 'OK, I trust that Aurora and Tempest will see us right.'

'Ella! Lola Faith! Hold on!' I called out, waving.

They looked up and smiled in relief, even as a massive gust of wind rocked their sleigh.

Aurora and Tempest swooped us in closer. Gramps and I leaned over and held out our hands.

'Now!' Gramps shouted.

Ella leaped and I grabbed her hand. Lola Faith did the same and Gramps caught her wrist. Together, we pulled them into our sleigh.

CRASH!

Below us, their sleigh toppled into the abyss.

We hovered for a moment in stunned silence, but soon Tempest and Aurora were racing back through the ice passageway and up and out of the fog.

We didn't speak until we saw blue sky.

'That was close,' said Ella, voice shaking.

'Too close,' said Lola Faith, wiping away a tear. 'I don't know what I would have done if my apo had been hurt. Thank you both so much for rescuing us.'

'What happened?' I asked. 'You were in the lead!'

'We were,' Ella said, 'but the map started acting real strange and then the next thing we knew we were at the Ice Cliffs. The wind blew us one way and our reindeer another, and the reins got torn by a sharp rock.' Ella bit her lip. 'I hope they're OK.'

Tempest and Aurora gave a whinny from the front and I wondered if they were saying that the reindeer were fine.

'I'm sure they got away,' I told Ella. 'I bet they've made their way back to the stables.'

Lola Faith looked at us curiously and said, 'What were *you two* doing at the Ice Cliffs.'

Gramps shrugged. 'Our map told us that you

were in trouble, so we came to get you.'

'You mean you completely blew your chances to win the challenge by rescuing us?' said Ella.

Like Gramps, I just shrugged. 'You were in danger – we *had* to help.'

'It was very Santa of you two, I think,' said Ella, beaming at me and Gramps.

Lola Faith wrapped my hand in hers. 'I agree! Not everyone would have acted as the Merrimans have done today! I kept thinking about how selfish it was for me to let Ella come along. I mean, with all that's going on at home, getting stranded on an ice cliff is the last thing our family needs.'

'What's wrong at home?' I asked, then bit my lip, wondering if I was being too nosy.

'It's OK,' said Ella. 'My little brother, Erwin, is sick. He's been waiting for a kidney transplant. It will help him get better.'

'We don't even know when the call will come,' added Lola Faith. 'But Ella was desperate to come

to Christmasland. And so was I . . . I thought maybe we both needed this, if only for a short while.'

'I get it,' Gramps said. 'And you deserve to be here, Faith.'

'We *all* deserve to be here,' Ella agreed. Then she whispered to me, 'But . . . I think someone tampered with our map.'

I frowned. 'What?'

Ella put a finger to her lips. 'Don't say anything to the grown-ups – at least not until we have evidence – but I'm sure someone messed with our map. The ink kept shifting about.'

'The same happened to us,' I said quietly.

Ella's eyes widened. 'We need to look out for our grandparents. Be careful who you trust.'

I nodded. Perhaps the other Hopefuls were hiding secrets or were playing dirty. If that was true, they had messed with the wrong grandkids.

More worried about keeping us safe than completing the challenge, Gramps tried to steer

us back to the village square, but it seemed that Aurora and Tempest didn't want us to give up. They whizzed through the air, finding the shortcut through Mistletoe Woods that they'd used before, and we were soon at the Candy Cane of Destiny. Having grabbed the last two wooden reindeer ornaments, to prove that we'd reached it, we wasted no time in heading back to the others.

The sky was thick with purple-grey clouds by the time we landed in the village square. Garlands of tiny fairy lights swayed in the air, twinkling brightly as we walked towards Chief Elf.

He pressed the button on the stopwatch hanging around his neck and looked at us sternly. 'Four people in one sleigh, Mr Merriman? That's hardly regulation.'

Smiling, Gramps and Lola Faith held up their wooden reindeer.

'At least we completed the task,' Gramps said.

'And it wasn't easy.' Ella climbed out the sleigh

and told Chief Elf in one breath about the Ice Cliffs and the reins snapping and being rescued from the falling sleigh.

Chief Elf barely blinked.

'Joint last,' he said, scribbling on his clipboard. He then radioed the stables and nodded tersely before telling us that Lola Faith and Ella's reindeer had got back safely.

'Lunch is in the Decked Halls,' he said as Ella and Lola Faith hugged each other in relief on hearing the reindeer were OK. 'Hurry along now – the others returned a while ago.'

With that, he stomped away.

I frowned. Something about his reaction didn't seem right – in fact, he'd hardly reacted at all. Ella thought someone was cheating. What if it wasn't a Hopeful? After all, how would a human know how to tamper with a magical map? What if it was someone on the *inside*?

11

WE FOLLOWED THE TRAIL OF FAIRY LIGHTS to the Decked Halls. The heavy oak door was decorated with a wreath of red ribbons and, as we stepped inside, the scent of roast potatoes hit me like a warm hug.

The hall was lined with miniature Christmas trees, glittering with silver, gold and metallic blue tinsel. A long table ran down the middle of the hall, heavy with food: roast turkey and stuffing, crispy prawns, tartlets and piles of roasted vegetables. No rice and peas or jollof,

though. We always have those at Christmas time at home.

I took the two last empty seats at the far end of the table, opposite Ella and Lola Faith. To our right were Chad and Jackson. Bram and Thomas were already tucking in.

Sophia grabbed a breadstick, holding it up like a microphone. 'Live from Christmasland, it's Sophia Moore!' she called. 'We've got Becka Moore in the house. Ms Moore, how does it feel being the first to snag a wooden reindeer from the Candy Cane of Destiny?'

Becka tossed her hair over her shoulder and gave a smile that somehow seemed stiff. 'I could never have done it without my awesome niece, Sophia!'

Sophia beamed. 'Overtaking Chad and

Jackson was definitely one for the books, Auntie Becka.' They both picked up their pink lemonade and clinked glasses.

'You won?' Ella asked, eyes wide.

'Yes, and in spectacular fashion too,' said Becka, smirking. 'No doubt we'll be headline news real soon when I become the next Santa.'

'Turns out being amazing at riding horses gives you a great instinct for working with reindeer,' said Sophia. 'We were slow to start and then *BAM!*' She thumped the table, making the cutlery clatter. 'We snatched up our reindeer and raced back. Chad and Jackson were just behind us.'

'Very well done,' said Gramps, even as Jackson scowled at Sophia and Becka.

'We were disappointed not to hold our lead,' Chad said smoothly, adjusting his cuffs, 'but Becka and Sophia won fair and square.'

'What happened to you lot?' Jackson asked,

gesturing at me, Gramps, Ella and Lola Faith with his fork. 'You were gone ages.'

'We ran into a little trouble, but Mikey and his grandfather helped us out,' Ella replied.

'Bad luck,' said Jackson with a snort. 'So joint last place.'

'There'll be other challenges,' I said, forcing a smile. 'We'll win the next one.'

I scanned the table, looking at everyone's faces. If someone had tampered with our map or Ella and Lola Faith's map, I needed them to think we didn't suspect a thing.

'I'm guessing you guys had trouble with your map then. Us too,' said Becka. 'I don't think it's very safe that Santa's people are handing out faulty maps. Good thing Sophia's a natural, or we'd still be out there in that fog.'

'Ah, that fog was awful,' said Mina, returning to the table with her dessert. She had a giant slice of chocolate cake on her plate. 'We got lost but

saw lots of Christmasland. We found the Candy Cane of Destiny eventually, though.'

'It was our very own adventure,' Tara said. 'So much fun.'

Mina gave her mum a high-five with chocolate-covered fingers.

"I'm not sure these words "lost" and "fun" go together,' Bram grumbled, playing with his spotless fork. 'Our reindeer only wanted to go round in circles.'

'It was very unfortunate,' Thomas Reijnders said, twirling his moustache, 'but character-building, Bram. I just don't think we ever unearthed the reindeer's true motivation for pulling the sleigh.'

Ella tapped my foot under the table and gave a tiny nod towards the drinks fountain, before standing up and heading over to it. I followed. She filled two glasses with lemonade and passed me one.

'Did you hear Becka and Sophia say they had problems with the map?' she whispered.

'Yeah,' I said, 'but I thought it was a humble brag.'

'Or a double bluff,' Ella said. 'What if they'd messed with our maps?'

I glanced back at the table. Becka was whispering something to Sophia, who nodded eagerly.

'Yeah, something about them is a bit suss,' I said, 'but I can't quite put my finger on why.'

'We need to watch them,' Ella said.

I raised my glass. 'To being watchful.'

'And to dessert,' said Ella. 'Things always look better after dessert.'

Chad and Jackson were deep in conversation about sleigh-riding strategies when we returned to the table with our pudding. Their ideas sounded really complicated.

Gramps had a hot drink and a wistful

expression. I sniffed the air. Chocolate, milk, cinnamon and nutmeg – his and Gran's cocoa tea recipe had somehow made its way to Christmasland!

I squeezed his arm. 'You OK, Gramps?'

'I'm OK, Mikey,' replied Gramps, blinking rapidly before forcing a smile. 'It's been an eventful day so far, that's all. I wish I could tell your gran about it.'

GONG! GONG!

Chief Elf appeared at the foot of the table with a thick bronze disc that was the same size as him.

The Decked Hall fell silent.

'Dear Hopefuls and Helpers,' announced Chief Elf. 'Santa extends his best wishes and cordially invites you to his Grotto. Please, follow me.'

Gramps bolted straight out of his seat. 'Santa's Grotto, Mikey! Can you believe it?!' He was bouncing on his heels as he waited for me to put on my coat.

We followed Chief Elf outside. Gramps was excitedly telling me all about how he and Gran always managed to make the community grotto look amazing with a bit of clever lighting and props – and tons of Blu Tack. He described how they'd convinced our local toyshop and bookshop to donate presents to the community grotto every year for kids who might otherwise not have any presents to open on Christmas Day.

'Why doesn't Santa get presents to all kids?' I asked Gramps.

Gramps looked thoughtful. 'The world is a complicated place, Mikey, and magic can only do so much, but I bet he tries. I bet he tries really hard.'

12

SANTA'S GROTTO WAS A HUGE LOG CABIN with red wooden trim and a chimney that puffed glittering clouds of multicoloured smoke. As we walked up the winding path that led to it, I could see that it was surrounded by carved wooden animals wearing Christmassy jumpers, hats and scarves.

Inside, the cabin was warm and cosy and smelled of roasted chestnuts and vanilla. A fire crackled in the hearth, and huge baubles glowed on the Christmas tree.

'Welcome, welcome!' Santa said. 'It is lovely to see you again.'

The Hopefuls and the Helpers all waved.

'I wonder what's through there?' murmured Gramps, nodding at a door with a blazing red 'RESTRICTED ACCESS' sign stretched across it.

'What lies beyond that door, Curtis Merriman, is a trade secret,' said Santa, tapping his nose.

Gramps stiffened. He hadn't meant Santa to hear! 'Um . . . Oh! I didn't mean to be nosy—'

'Oh, ho ho ho! Why, curiosity is a natural hallmark of Santa!' His eyes twinkled merrily behind his gold-rimmed glasses. 'In that room, which you are forbidden to enter, we keep magical formulas created by Santas Past. It is through their wit and imagination and, of course, curiosity that the elves and I are able to craft so many toys and deliver them in a single night.'

'Oh, pleeeeease, Santa!' Mina begged. 'Please can we have a look inside?'

Chief Elf stepped forward, all serious and frowning. 'The contents of that room are extremely TOP SECRET.' He crossed his arms.

'I've said too much already.' Santa nodded solemnly. 'But only the next Santa will get to find out what's in there.'

Mina smiled hopefully at her mum. Jackson nudged Chad, while Becka high-fived Sophia. Thomas and Bram were staring at the door with so much curiosity it was as if they were trying to activate X-ray vision. I looked at Gramps and wondered what he was thinking – but his expression was giving nothing away.

We followed Santa and Chief Elf through to a storeroom that stretched several floors upwards, where rows of puzzles and dolls and robots and board games were neatly stacked, waiting for their Christmas Eve delivery.

WHOOOOSH!

An elf whizzed up one of the top shelves and

placed a cuddly teddy bear next to a fidget spinner before speeding back out of the room again.

'Ooh – I bet that was just made in Santa's Workshop!' Ella whispered to me, peering around to see where the elf had gone, but I nudged her in the direction of Chad Buckles instead. We watched as he sternly told Jackson to take a video game out of his pocket and put it back on its shelf.

We entered Santa's Den, a small room with humongous armchairs that surrounded a roaring fireplace. In the middle of the space was a large table with drinks and snacks, as well as a leader board with six miniature sleighs lined up at the bottom.

I blinked and looked closer – there were little figures moving inside the sleighs! I spotted me and Gramps, waving at the real me in excitement.

Santa cleared his throat. 'Now, while the official decision for the next Santa rests with

me, Chief Elf thought it would be helpful to mark each Hopeful's progress on the Santa Search leader board.'

Becka practically shoved me out of the way as she rushed to push her miniature sleigh to the very top of the board. Chad placed his sleigh as closely behind Becka's as possible. Tara's was moved to third position, and Thomas in fourth. Ella and I positioned our sleighs next to each other at the very end.

I glanced anxiously at Santa, hoping he wouldn't be too disappointed in me and Gramps. I wanted to let him know we were serious candidates, but the moment I edged closer to Santa, Chief Elf shot me a warning frown.

Chief Elf was high on my list of possible saboteurs. It was clear he didn't want anyone getting too friendly with Santa, but was he following official protocol, or had he figured out that I was suspicious of him?

'How about that leader board, huh? Looks pretty sweet with us at the top!' Sophia crowed.

'At this rate, we'll be unlocking the secret room in no time,' Becka said, giving her niece a wink.

'Only the winner may enter, you know,' Bram said, frowning.

'Bram, it's obvious *we're* going to be crowned as winners,' retorted Sophia.

'All kinds of things are obvious when you *really* look,' said Santa. 'Becka Moore, congratulations on winning the navigation task!' he continued. 'Please, take a seat with me by the fire.'

Becka sat with Santa, while Sophia lounged comfortably on the side of her aunt's armchair. It was clear they believed they had already won and were getting very comfortable in Santa's grotto.

'Was that the first time you drove a sleigh?' Santa asked. 'By all accounts, you were professionals!'

'Why, thank you!' said Becka, flicking her hair over her shoulders. 'No, we hadn't so much as seen a sleigh before in our lives. Though it's my niece, Sophia, who's the professional horse rider and that certainly helped.'

'I go horse riding every week back home. It was no big deal.' Sophia shrugged. 'I mean, there's not much difference between reindeer and horses, right?'

'Hmm,' said Santa, stroking his beard thoughtfully. 'Appearances can be deceptive, but please do go on and tell me your strategy. How did you win the task?'

Becka launched into a very long description, and I heard Ella yawn next to me.

'It's so warm in here,' she muttered. 'Aren't you feeling sleepy?'

'A little bit,' I said, stifling my own yawn. 'I think it's the heat.'

'Or maybe it's because I've lost count of how

many times Becka and Sophia have bragged about their win in the last hour,' said Ella.

I laughed at that. It was true. Becka had hardly paused for breath. I looked over at her. Surely she would stop talking soon.

Wait.

Becka looked different. Really different.

I rubbed my eyes and blinked, then rubbed them again.

Becka Moore's face was melting right in front of our eyes!

13

THE CONVERSATION IN THE ROOM STOPPED.

Sophia leaped off the armchair and gave a squeal of horror.

'What's going on?' asked Becka.

'Auntie B, it's your—'

Santa held up a hand to stop Sophia. His eyes were fixed firmly on Becka as he fanned her with a newspaper he'd picked up from a nearby table.

'You know, I read the most extraordinary article this morning,' Santa began, unfolding the newspaper with a loud rustle. 'It was all about

Christmasland, written by a journalist called Beatrice Bolt. It was mentioned that she was here with her horse-mad niece. Chief Elf, do tell me – do we know anyone by the name of Beatrice Bolt here in Christmasland?'

Chief Elf shook his head. 'No one has registered under that name, Santa.'

'How strange,' murmured Santa, watching as Becka and Sophia stiffened. 'Perhaps this will enlighten us all.'

Santa opened the newspaper to reveal an article headlined 'SNOOTY ELVES AND DANGEROUS CARRIAGES: OUR FIRST NIGHT UNDERCOVER IN CHRISTMASLAND'. My mouth dropped open at the photograph of the Moores, which had been taken in front of the Snowflake Wheel.

Becka – or Beatrice – opened her mouth to speak, but her nose slid off her face and landed on the floor with a loud plop.

'OK, OK, you got me!' Becka said resentfully, yanking off a blonde wig to reveal a short brown bob underneath. 'My real name is Beatrice Bolt and I'm an award-winning investigative journalist! If it wasn't for that foolish editor of mine publishing this too early, you wouldn't have guessed my true identity. But you know what? I don't even care, because I am SICK of wearing that wig and face mask!'

'So why were you wearing it then?' I asked, feeling confused.

'*Because* I am very famous and I may have been recognised.' Becka – no, Beatrice glared at me impatiently. 'I was offered a big fee to go undercover and report on Christmasland. It's in the public interest for us to know exactly what goes on here, and there's no good reason it should be a secret at all.'

Santa neatly folded the newspaper and set it on his lap. Beatrice had raised her chin, trying to

look proud of herself, but I noticed she couldn't quite meet Santa's intense stare.

'Were you aware of this plot too, Sophia?' Santa asked quietly, his cheerful voice now tinged with disappointment.

Sophia gulped. 'Yes, but only because Auntie Beatrice promised to buy me a pony for Christmas. I ask for one *every year* and I never get it.'

Santa looked thoughtful for a moment. 'Sophia, do you remember the pony plushie I gave you for Christmas?'

'Yeah, when I was six. I called her Snorsey.' Sophia's voice was rather small. 'I brought her with me to Christmasland. I can't fall asleep without her.' Guilt and regret was written all over Sophia's face, even if she couldn't quite bring herself to say sorry.

Santa smiled sadly at her. 'I hope you get what you want this Christmas, dear Sophia, but I hope

even more that you leave Christmasland with an appreciation for the true magic of this season – one that has nothing to do with ticking off items on your wish list. Take care. I hope the next Santa will see you and Snorsey again very soon.'

A grave-faced Sugar Plum emerged from a corner.

'Let's go,' she said, and led Sophia and Beatrice out of Christmasland forever.

Ella leaned in and whispered, 'If they lied about who they were, they're probably the ones who messed with our map, right?'

I nodded slowly. The signs had been there all along. But, even though they were gone, I couldn't shake the unease clinging to me.

'Well,' Thomas said, hands clasped behind his back, 'what an interesting insight into the workings of deception.'

'And our chances have improved considerably,' Chad added.

Jackson snorted. 'One down. Four to go. One to win.'

Mina Bakhshi frowned. 'That's not very Christmassy of you.'

'It's a competition,' Jackson said with a shrug. 'What? You think the next Santa will be based on who sings the most carols?'

'Not exactly,' said Santa, standing now, his expression unreadable. 'But I do look for the kind of person who embodies the Christmas spirit – someone who is determined, yes, but also cares for others, who tells the truth, who does the right thing even when it's hard.'

Chad flashed a grin as if Santa was describing him.

'Jackson just cares too much,' said Chad. 'It can come across as being rather rumbunctious, but he is the kindest and most honest of souls.' I noticed how Jackson shifted uncomfortably at those words.

'Let me be absolutely clear,' Chief Elf said, staring at all of us. 'Deception has no place in Christmasland.'

I froze. My heart hammered. Had he been looking at *me* when he said that? I hadn't lied to win. Not really. I'd only bent the rules to get Gramps here. It wasn't the same . . .

But the twisty feeling in my stomach said otherwise.

'Good,' Chief Elf said at last. 'Then we move on. The next challenge awaits. Please follow me to the arena.'

Santa waved goodbye – a little sadly, I thought – as we trailed after Chief Elf. When we passed the leader board, I couldn't help but glance at it. Beatrice and Sophia's sleigh had vanished and the board had been updated:

1ST

CHAD AND JACKSON BUCKLES

2ND

TARA AND MINA BAKHSHI

3RD

THOMAS AND BRAM REIJNDERS

4TH & 5TH

FAITH AND ELLA DIAZ;

CURTIS AND MIKEY MERRIMAN

Gramps nudged me gently. 'It's not over yet, Mikey, and remember: we're here for the fun, not for the win.'

I nodded, but I still felt the weight of everything I hadn't told Gramps.

A CHEERY ELF IN A TARTAN TRACKSUIT WAS waiting for us outside an enormous round building with high walls.

'Good afternoon, Santa's Hopefuls and Helpers! I'm Merry, and I am delighted to be leading the second Santa Search challenge today – wild reindeer taming!'

Bram and Thomas Reijnders looked at each other in horror.

'The instructions are as follows,' continued Merry, her voice as soothing as cough syrup.

'Tame a wild reindeer and ride it round the arena once. Extra points if you can make it fly!'

'I think we're in with a good chance here, Mikey,' said Gramps, his eyes lighting up. 'We're not bad with reindeer, are we?'

'No, Gramps – I'd say we're *excellent* with reindeer,' I replied, grinning.

I didn't want to get my hopes up, but I felt that Gramps might actually be warming to the idea of winning Santa Search.

'Now,' said Merry, clasping her hands together, 'you've all had a chance to bond with the sleigh reindeer. Anyone care to share what you noticed?'

Mina shot her hand up. 'They smelled like caramel on vanilla ice cream!'

'They're brave and loyal,' added Ella. 'Apparently, ours spent ages trying to find us after we got separated from them.'

'They're fast,' Jackson said with a smirk, 'if you know how to handle them properly.'

'They are stubborn, those reindeer,' Bram muttered. 'Ours, they did not listen at all.' He rubbed a hand over his face. 'I can't believe we are doing reindeer again,' he added with a sigh. 'There must be more to being Santa than just dealing with them!'

Merry raised an eyebrow. 'Truth be told, there is a lot of reindeer action in the job.'

Bram snorted in disgust and Thomas looked rather worried.

Merry turned to Gramps. 'And you? What did you learn about reindeer?'

'I learned they are magnificent,' said Gramps, smiling broadly. 'Absolutely magnificent.'

Merry beamed. 'Aurora and Tempest had kind things to say about you too.' Then, with a swift movement, she pulled out a gold megaphone and shouted, 'Now forget EVERYTHING you think you know about reindeer!'

We jumped. Even Chief Elf seemed startled.

Merry began pacing back and forth. 'Wild reindeer are NOTHING like sleigh reindeer. They smell like rotten eggs, they won't take orders, and they're loyal to no one but themselves. If they sense a hint of disrespect . . . you'd better hope the medic elves are quick to the rescue.'

'Well, as you mention it,' said Chad Buckles, stepping forward with Jackson, 'may we take this opportunity to say that we have brought some extra safety equipment.'

'I've been studying wild reindeer,' Jackson added smoothly. 'We anticipated this, so we packed protective armour.'

Chad clicked his fingers and two elves appeared with shiny black cases.

'Wait. How'd they do that?' Gramps asked. 'I didn't know we could click for elves.'

'You can't,' Merry said as she watched Chad and Jackson unpack glinting breastplates and

reinforced gloves, as well as foam padding to go under the armour.

'Even elves need pocket money,' Jackson explained.

I glanced down at my bomber jacket and snow boots. Not exactly battle-ready. Gramps looked even less prepared in his old woollen coat and flat cap.

'Excellent initiative, Buckles family!' said Chief Elf, scribbling on his clipboard.

I sighed inwardly and kicked myself. I'd packed my toothbrush, but I could've brought Mum's old boxing gloves or our cycling helmets too.

'You'll be fine, Mikey,' Ella whispered. 'Lola and I don't have armour either.'

'Yeah,' I said, 'But your lola used to be a vet. I bet she's going to be great with wild reindeer.'

'My mum's tamed twenty rescue cats,' Mina chimed in. 'It was her hobby for a bit. They were feral and mean, but she won them over. It's about

respect and reading cues. If we remember that, no one will get hurt.'

'Hurt?' said Bram, his voice cracking.

'Don't worry,' Thomas said gently. 'Just stay close to me.'

We followed Merry inside the huge building, which turned out to be a vast, circular stadium ringed with candy-striped stands. Hundreds of elves munched on popcorn and toffee apples, and some held banners that had our names on.

'*AAAAAND HERE THEY COME – SANTA'S HOPEFULS!*' bellowed a voice from the speakers. '*TIME FOR A WILD DANCE WITH DESTINY!*'

A roar of applause followed.

'*Today, five Hopefuls will attempt to tame wild reindeer. Will it end in disaster or delight?*' said the commentator.

'DISASTER!' shouted half the crowd.

'DELIGHT!' yelled the other half.

'*In the arena are Chad Buckles, Faith Diaz, Thomas Reijnders, Curtis Merriman and Tara Bakhshi! Earlier today, Beatrice Bolt was disqualified for DECEPTION!*'

A large screen flashed awake, showing Becka-now-Beatrice's face as it melted into her true identity.

'BOOOOOO!' howled the elves, pumping their fists angrily in the air.

On-screen, a giant black boot swung into view and kicked Beatrice's figure out of sight.

The crowd whooped.

I spotted Sugar Plum in the front row, and she gave us a thumbs up. Santa sat beside her, clapping eagerly as Chief Elf walked over to join them. I gulped. Losing was one thing – losing in front of Santa was worse.

'Listen closely!' Merry barked to us. 'When the jingle bells ring, each team will enter the arena from a separate entrance. Once inside the arena,

the door locks behind you, the spectator shields will go up, and then we release the wild reindeer.'

'What's that?' Bram pointed towards a tent at the arena's edge. It was red and white, and had stretchers stacked outside.

'Medic tent,' said Merry. 'You *probably* won't need it.'

Thomas shook his head. 'This is rather outrageous – I'm not sure about this. Shouldn't you have stunt people to do this kind of work?'

Merry held his gaze. 'This is not a film set, Mr Reijnders. The choice is yours to continue or not.'

Bram tugged his dad's sleeve. 'Come on, we've got this far. And remember what you said – the critics are going to love the fact that you got beneath the skin of the role.'

I frowned. What did Bram mean by that? And how come I could understand their whispered conversation in Dutch? *It must be Christmasland magic.*

Merry escorted Gramps and me inside, and we faced our door to the arena.

Jingle, jingle, jingle. The bell had sounded.

'We might not have armour, but we have each other,' I said, reaching for the handle.

But Gramps blocked the door. 'No, Mikey.

It's too dangerous. I don't know what Santa was thinking, but you're not going in there.'

'Wh-what?' I spluttered. 'Gramps, we're a team! What if you need me?'

Gramps shook his head. 'I'd never forgive myself if you got hurt. I've lost too much this year.'

And, quick as a flash, he stepped through the door and shut it firmly behind him.

'No!' I shouted, banging the door. If I wasn't going out there, Gramps shouldn't be out there either. I tried to wrench the door open, but it was locked fast.

'I'm afraid that once the door is shut, there's no reopening it until the challenge is over,' Merry gently reminded me. 'Remember, there is always a choice, and your grandfather made his. You'll have to watch from the stands.'

15

I RAN AND FOUND AN ARCHWAY THAT LED TO
the stadium seats. I squeezed past a throng of
jostling elves and pushed my way to the front.

The Spectator Shield flickered in front of me,
keeping me out of the arena, but I put my nose
right up to it. I could see the other Hopefuls and
Helpers. And Gramps all alone.

The commentator's voice thundered across
the arena. '*On your marks . . . Get set . . . Release!*'

The gates flew open and five wild reindeer
stampeded out.

My breath caught. These weren't anything like sleigh reindeer. They were giants – antlers sharp and eyes glowing amber. Muscles rippled under their shaggy coats. One of them barrelled straight towards Gramps. He held out his hands in a calming gesture, but the reindeer just snorted, hooves crashing on the hard ground.

'GRAMPS, WATCH OUT!' I shouted.

The spectators in the crowd gasped as Gramps jumped out of the way at the last second and the reindeer changed course to charge around the arena.

Gramps staggered to his feet. His eyes met mine through the shield.

He was afraid.

And so was I.

The other Hopefuls were making better progress. Tara had fed her wild reindeer a cookie, and now it was happily licking crumbs off her and Mina's palms.

Ella had been right about her lola's skill with animals. Lola Faith was calmly stroking their reindeer's neck and murmuring softly, while the creature stood obediently beside them. It even gave a slight tail swish as Lola Faith rubbed its flank.

As for the Buckles, Chad and Jackson were working the crowd like professionals. They juggled carrots in perfect sync, flashing identical grins and tossing an occasional carrot to their admiring reindeer, who watched with mesmerised honey-brown eyes.

I felt a sharp twist in my gut. That could've been me and Gramps. If I'd prepared better. If he'd let me go into the arena with him. I felt so annoyed that he hadn't taken me. Instead, I was stuck behind this shield, completely helpless as Gramps struggled to keep out of the way of a really angry reindeer.

Gramps stumbled, slipping on a patch of ice,

but he kept his balance and carried on moving.

'What's the plan, Gramps?' I said out loud.

'Aaaaaaaaaargh!'

A cry tore through the air.

Bram and Thomas Reijnders had been cornered. Their wild reindeer loomed above them, steam billowing from its nostrils. Thomas and Bram had retreated so far that their backs were pressed flat against the Spectator Shield.

The reindeer twitched its nose. Then . . .
ACHOOOO!

A huge glob of luminous yellow snot exploded from its snout, landing directly on their faces. It slithered down in thick, gooey blobs like custard.

I gagged. That was utterly gross.

'Oh no!' the commentator cried. 'It looks like the Reijnders are having a *truly revolting* time! That's a five-blob sneeze, folks – our highest ever rating!'

The arena screen replayed the sneeze in

slow motion, complete with a banner that read: 'SLIME TIME!'

'That's it!' Thomas cried as the reindeer shook its head after its massive sneeze. 'I'm an award-winning actor and no role is worth this!' His eyes were wild. 'I thought I could make Santa sophisticated again, mysterious – but This. Is. A. Joke. *Santa is a joke.*'

His words echoed around the arena as he marched towards the doors on the opposite side.

Gasps rippled through the crowd. The camera found Santa, and his hurt expression was broadcast on the screen for all to see.

'BOOOOOOO!' howled the elves, stamping their boots and shaking empty popcorn tubs.

But it wasn't just the elves that were displeased.

Thomas's reindeer turned, pawed the ground, then charged forward with terrifying speed.

Thomas glanced over his shoulder, slipped on

the snowy ground and tried to regain his balance, but it was too late.

The reindeer dipped its head and scooped him up from behind with its antlers, flipping Thomas with a single powerful toss.

'AAAAAAARGHHHH!'

Thomas spun through the air like a rag doll in a padded winter coat – once, twice, three times. Two medic elves dashed towards him with a stretcher, catching him right before he landed. In a blink, they whisked him off to the medic tent.

Bram, still slimed with snot, followed with a dazed look.

'I am NEVER coming back to Christmasland!' he wailed.

'That's probably for the best,' muttered the elf next to me, nudging his tub of popcorn my way. 'Hello there. My name's Bauble but call me Bill. Fancy a nibble?'

I shook my head, my eyes fixed on Gramps. He was backed up against the Spectator Shield as his reindeer approached. Was he going to get slimed like Thomas?

'Tame it! You can do this, Gramps!' I yelled, even though I wasn't sure he could.

'Oh, jolly candlesticks!' Bill exclaimed. 'He's your grandfather, is he? Think he's about to get slimed.' Bill shook his head sadly before stuffing more popcorn in his mouth.

Gramps unwrapped his scarf and held it aloft, in front of his face.

The reindeer tilted its head to one side and watched him curiously.

Gramps peered up at the reindeer, then waved his scarf in front of the beast as if he was a matador.

'Has he got wild reindeer confused with bulls?' Bill asked. 'I don't think reindeer like scarves. They don't like much, really . . . other than music, I suppose.'

I groaned. 'What are you doing, Gramps?'

The reindeer gave a long, rumbling disapproving snort.

'Told you,' Bill said.

The other reindeer in the arena started pawing

the ground and all turned to face Gramps. Ella and Lola Faith tried to distract their reindeer, but it was no good. Luckily, Mina and Tara's reindeer was fast asleep.

The air changed. As if the whole arena was holding its breath.

'I've got to stop him!' I shouted at Bill. 'He's making it worse!'

'Not much you nor I can do,' Bill replied cheerfully.

My hands curled into fists. Gramps had locked me out to keep me safe. He thought this was something he had to do alone. But he was wrong. This was never meant to be a solo mission. We were in this together.

'Hold on, Gramps,' I whispered. 'I'm coming.'

16

I HAD TO THINK FAST. I TURNED TO BILL AND
said, 'Is there any way I can get past the
Spectator Shield? *Any* way at all!'

Bill was silent for a moment. 'Actually! We
love to chuck satsumas at riders we don't like,'
he said cheerfully. 'See that gap over on the left?
They forgot to patch it after last year's derby
– the one where the Arctic Aerialists and the
Soaring Stars both tried to land on the same yak.
That whole section collapsed like a badly made
gingerbread house.'

I was already scrambling down towards it when he called after me, 'Just don't tell Chief Elf I told you, OK?'

'Thanks, Bill! It's our secret!'

I spotted Santa across the arena. He winked at me as I approached the gap in the shield, but Chief Elf hadn't noticed me at all.

I wriggled through the gap and into the arena.

'Oi! Reindeer! I've got something to tell you,' I bellowed, running as fast as I could towards Gramps.

The wild reindeer all turned to face me.

The ground shook beneath my feet as the creatures charged towards me – a storm of muscle and fur. The hair on the back of my neck tickled. I could smell the wild reindeer on the wind. They definitely didn't smell of vanilla or caramel. Everything went still.

I opened my mouth and started singing. Bill said they liked music, right?

'*Brown reindeer in the ring, tra la la la la . . . There's a brown reindeer in the ring . . .*'

The wild reindeer slowed from a gallop to a trot, listening. Gramps scrambled to my side.

'What are you doing here, Mikey?'

'Later, Gramps,' I gasped. 'We need to sing. Wild reindeer like music!'

'*There's a brown reindeer in the ring . . .*' Gramps began.

'Louder, Gramps!' I urged.

'*Tra la la la la!*' Gramps's deep baritone filled the arena. Then he even started to dance.

'How extraordinary . . . Curtis and Mikey Merriman's song appears to be *calming* the wild reindeer!' the commentator cried.

The reindeer who had been Gramps's nemesis came right up to us and dipped his head. I realised it was an invitation. I took a breath and clambered onto the reindeer's back.

Boy, this reindeer was smelly.

'Mikey!' Gramps croaked.

'Keep singing, Gramps, and get on. This is the right thing to do, I know it,' I said.

We began singing together as Gramps scrambled up behind me.

'*SHOW ME YOUR MOTION . . . Tra la la la la!*'

The wild reindeer began to canter and then sped up to gallop round the arena.

'Don't stop singing!' I shouted. '*SHOW ME YOUR MOTION . . . Tra la la la la la . . .*'

'Mikey, we'd better jump off . . . *Tra la la la la!*' Gramps sang quickly. '*A brown reindeer in the ring . . .* is going to crash into the Spectator Shield . . . *tra la la la la la!*'

'Whooooooaaaaaa!' I cried as we suddenly took to the air. I felt weightless.

'We're flying!' Gramps gasped in disbelief, but then gave a hoot of delighted laughter.

The wild reindeer snorted happily as Gramps and I soared above the arena.

'We did it, Gramps!' I whooped, patting the reindeer on its neck. It didn't smell that badly now the air was whistling past my face.

Multicoloured dots bopped in the stands below us as elves cheered and clapped and punched their fists in the air.

Our wild reindeer gracefully weaved through the sky in a figure of eight and the crowd roared with enthusiasm below.

'Hang on a minute . . .' I paused, listening. 'Gramps! The elves aren't cheering. They're singing your song!'

'Our song, Mikey,' Gramps said. 'I'm sorry I left you. Losing Claudette broke my heart. I was worried about you getting hurt and I panicked.'

I nodded, my throat feeling a bit tight. I understood now why he did what he did.

'We're a team, Gramps.'

'Always,' Gramps replied.

Calmed and uplifted by the singing audience,

our wild reindeer swooped in another elegant loop. It had never been a monster, after all – it just had a lot of energy that we needed to put to good use.

At last, we landed gently on the ground, where the crowd greeted us with a standing ovation.

'SIMPLY OUTSTANDING!' the commentator boomed. 'An absolutely *unmatched* display of TRUE CHRISTMAS SPIRIT! What a marvel Curtis and Mikey Merriman are!'

The wild reindeer kneeled down, letting Gramps and I gingerly step off it.

'Mikey Boy, that was one of the most incredible experiences I've ever had!' Gramps said, pulling me in for a hug.

Chief Elf walked over to us, swiftly scribbling something on his clipboard.

'Third place,' he said curtly. 'For the time it took and the lack of expertise shown by your team initially. However, you were the only team to fly.' He paused and glanced at us. 'Very well done for

realising that wild reindeer may be soothed by a melody that is full of heart. If only you hadn't taken so long to tame it!'

It might have been wishful thinking, but I thought Chief Elf's harsh tone had softened a little before he strode off.

A drumroll rumbled over the speakers.

'The results have been released!' the commentator announced.

'In first place with a total of twelve points we have . . . Chad and Jackson Buckles! This father-and-son duo impressed Chief Elf by managing to get their wild reindeer tamed and under control from the *very second* it entered the arena. Congratulations!'

'How did they do that?' I wondered out loud, frowning.

A recap of Chad and Jackson's success was shown on the big screen with big block letters that flashed: 'CAN'T BEAT THE BUCKLES!'

'Second place has been awarded to Faith and Ella Diaz!' the commentator continued. 'Their calming words quickly soothed their wild reindeer, earning them a new total of eight points.'

I gave Ella a thumbs up as she and Lola Faith bounced up and down with happiness.

'CUR-TIS! CUR-TIS!' the audience rumbled.

'You guessed it!' The commentator chuckled. 'They took their time but Curtis and Mikey Merriman are in third place for taming their wild reindeer with a sweet song that sent them flying. The song even got Santa on his feet! Seven points!'

Gramps and I watched ourselves on the screen as the crowd broke out in raucous applause.

'Should have got first!' I think I heard Merry say to my left.

'And, as you saw, Thomas and Bram Reijnders have withdrawn from the competition. Thomas wants it to be known that the rights to his story

are available to be acquired by interested publishers and he would star as himself in any film but he is no longer interested in playing Santa in the much-anticipated film *Santa's Last Dance.*'

The elves in the stand looked at each other in confusion. I was a bit confused myself to be honest, with all the talk of rights and publishers and films.

'Aaaand last but not least in this challenge . . . we have Tara and Mina Bakhshi in fourth place!' the commentator said. 'They were among the first to tame their wild reindeer . . . by putting it to sleep! However, Chief Elf has ruled that the reindeer must be awake for it to count as being tamed.'

Mina crossed her arms in annoyance, but her mum just gave her a hug and said, 'No drama, love. We're second overall in terms of points, and I reckon our reindeer really loved that bikkie.

It was real nice of Sugar Plum to give it to us.'

Seeing Tara comfort Mina suddenly made me feel homesick for Mum and Dad, and Gramps squeezed my shoulder, as if he knew.

'That's it, folks,' the commentator announced. 'Hope you've enjoyed the show!'

17

EVERYONE LOOKED DRAINED AND dishevelled as Chief Elf led us to the Decked Halls for our tea. Only Tara and Mina seemed perky as they raced over to the marvellous evening Christmas feast. I piled my plate high with roasted herb potatoes, honey salmon bites, green beans, carrots and parsnips. Taming wild reindeer was hungry work!

I sat next to Ella at the end of the long table, now laid with a burgundy tablecloth, shiny gold plates and flickering candles.

'Fancy some food with that gravy?' I joked, pointing at her plate. Bits of potato, roasted chicken and unidentifiable vegetables poked out of a sea of rich brown liquid.

'Gravy's not a big thing in Singapore, but I'm totally into it,' Ella said as she speared her fork into a gravy-soaked sprout.

'So . . . do you still think someone's sabotaging us?' I asked in a low voice.

Ella chewed her sprout thoughtfully. 'No, I don't. I'm pretty sure it was Becka – I mean Beatrice – tampering with our maps in some way. It makes sense, doesn't it? She faked her identity to write an undercover report on Christmasland, so she's clearly not the most truthful person and she wanted to create drama.' Ella grinned. 'Talking of drama, it was a lot watching you and your lolo in that arena.'

I laughed. 'Gramps totally crushed it!'

'Lolo Curtis is good,' Ella admitted, 'but not

quite as amazing as my lola.'

I smiled. Although Ella and Lola Faith were strong competition, I didn't see them as rivals. Just friends. If Gramps couldn't be Santa, I'd want it to be Lola Faith.

'How about Gramps and Lola Faith are, like, joint amazingest then?' I conceded.

'Deal,' Ella said, reaching out to fist-bump me. 'Although you do know there's no such word as "amazingest", right? You can take it from me – I speak three languages: English, Tagalog and a bit of Mandarin.'

'Fine,' I agreed. 'Come on, we'd better eat up. Apparently there is another challenge straight after this one.'

The Hopefuls and Helpers gathered in a cobbled courtyard outside the Clockmaker's Workshop –

a wide brick building with a steep tiled roof and a crooked chimney. Frost edged the windows, and from within came the soft, rhythmic ticking of clocks and the grind of hidden gears.

High on the front of the building were four large clock faces, each one frozen on a different time: one o'clock, two o'clock, three o'clock, and four o'clock. Beneath each clock stood a wooden door, shut fast.

Chief Elf stood between the two central doors, tapping on a thick stone tablet that glowed faintly with electric light. It looked like something ancient, though it blinked and beeped like a modern gadget.

'I have read in the human newspapers that there are "escape rooms" in your world, is that correct?' he asked.

Everyone nodded.

'Excellent,' Chief Elf continued. 'Inside this workshop are escape rooms. Each team will face

the rooms and the festive challenges contained within. Solve one room, and you'll be guided to the next. First team to finish all rooms is the winner.'

He lowered the tablet with a smile. 'And remember: it's important to pay attention to *everything*, all the small details. Teams that work together win together. Do take a moment to discuss your strategy with your companion.'

'You ready?' I asked Gramps.

I'm not sure I was. Escape rooms brought up weird feelings for me. Mum and Dad had booked one for my birthday earlier in the year because our family loves puzzles, but Gramps hadn't come. He said it didn't feel right having fun without Gran. He'd taken me out another day, though – just the two of us. But, still, I was worried this would bring back bad memories.

Gramps gave a small smile. 'Ready as I'll ever be.'

Then he paused. The smile faltered slightly.

'Mikey, before we go in – thank you. I know it's not been easy for any of us this past year. I have been dreading Christmas, you know. I think Christmas can be really hard for people who've lost loved ones . . . It can be hard for all kinds of people for all kinds of reasons. I know that Christmas won't ever be the same without Claudette. But maybe . . . it can still be special? We can still have fun?'

My throat felt tight. I reached for his hand and gave it a squeeze.

'Choose your door and take your path,' Chief Elf called out. 'On your marks . . . Get set . . . Go, go, go!'

Jackson Buckle raced to a door and muttered under his breath as he rattled it, but nothing happened.

It was the same for Mina. 'I think this door is broken, Chief Elf.'

I peered up at the building. The clocks, the numbers, the frozen times.

Something clicked.

'Hang on,' I said to Gramps. 'Look at the times. That one says four o'clock. And we're fourth on the leader board.'

Gramps followed my gaze. 'So the times on the clock refer to the position of the teams . . . You might be right, Mikey Boy.'

'Let's give it a try,' I said.

We walked to the four o'clock door and pushed the handle. There was a low mechanical click. The door swung open, spilling warm golden light into the cold night.

'Clever lad,' Gramps murmured.

The other teams started scrambling for their matching clocks. I pointed at the clock saying two o'clock to Ella. Though the Diazes and the Bakhshis both had eight points, Faith had won the last challenge, so I was sure her number would be

higher than Tara's. Then Gramps and I made our way inside.

The room looked like an old-fashioned parlour. It was all dark wood panelling and velvet curtains, with a pair of button-backed armchairs near a cast-iron stove. A tall Christmas tree stood proudly in the room, and it dripped with brass baubles and flickering candle-shaped lights. The tick of a wall clock echoed gently in the hush, and on one side of the room, rolls of wrapping paper were stacked neatly in a wooden rack – each roll tagged with a number. Next to it was a shelf filled with boxes, each with a numbered gift tag.

'Feels like stepping back in time,' said Gramps, running a hand along the smooth shelf of a bookcase.

'Gramps, over here!' I called.

Hanging low on the Christmas tree was a large wooden gift tag, polished and engraved.

I leaned in to read it aloud:

1. Wrap the presents as quickly as you can. Extra points will be awarded for neat and pleasant presentation.

2. Each present and roll of wrapping paper is numbered. Make sure they match.

3. Once wrapped, use the presents to solve the puzzle grid hidden somewhere in this room. The correct arrangement will reveal the code to unlock the next door.

'Let's go,' Gramps said, already heading for the paper rack.

We knew what we were doing. The Merrimans had been wrapping gifts at record speed for the grotto since I was old enough to hold a roll of tape. Gramps measured and cut the thick wrapping paper, while I wrapped and taped. We worked in sync, exactly like we had at Gran and Gramps's grotto back at the community centre. Paper, fold, tape, stick, done.

Within minutes, we had a stack of neatly wrapped boxes, each with its matching paper and number.

'Now for the puzzle,' said Gramps.

We searched the room carefully, checking drawers, tapping the walls and even lifting cushions. The ticking of the clock was getting louder and louder – I think we were running out of time.

Then I spotted the heavy rug on the floor.

'Let's check under here,' I said. 'Gramps, help me roll it back.'

Beneath it, carved directly into the floorboards, was a nine-square grid, and it was exactly the right size for the gifts. A number pattern was engraved beside it. Feeling excited,

we used it to work out where each box should go, moving them around until they matched.

The grid glowed white, and four of the presents began to vibrate. First number 6, then number 1, followed by 4, then 5.

'Yes!' I said, grinning. Gramps raised his hand and we high-fived. 'That must be the code!'

The ticking quietened. To the left of the stove, a brass keypad blinked to life. I punched in the code – 6145 – and held my breath.

There was a quiet click. The bookcase swung open – it was a secret door!

'Next room,' said Gramps.

And in we went.

18

ON THE OTHER SIDE OF THE DOOR WAS A kitchen that looked like it came from Victorian times. Gears and cranks were set into the wall and there was a clock above the fireplace.

We washed our hands as instructed by the notice next to the sink and put on the aprons that had been left out for us.

On a large, smooth wooden table the walls of a gingerbread house were neatly laid out. Beside them were several bowls of sweets and an icing bag. A handwritten note was propped against a pot containing one of those plants with the big red leaves. It read:

☆ Build your
gingerbread house,
but don't feel dread.

Just be careful to
mind your head! ☆

'How long do we have?' I asked, already reaching for the gingerbread walls.

'I don't know,' Gramps muttered, frowning and looking up. 'But unless I've had a sudden growth spurt, I think the ceiling dropped a little since we got here.'

I followed his gaze. He was right! The ceiling was definitely closer to the clock on the wall than it had been when we'd first entered. We both gulped.

There was no time to waste. Gramps grabbed the icing bag while I held the gingerbread pieces upright. The mechanical whir of the ceiling lowering got louder, and my hands began to tremble. I kept losing my grip.

We worked as fast as we could. Once the walls of the gingerbread house were up, we piped around the windows and door, then added gumdrops to decorate the roof. Gramps made a marshmallow snowman and looped strawberry laces round its neck like a scarf. I added the finishing flourishes, but still the ceiling kept dropping.

Whiirrrrrrrrr.

'Crouch down, Mikey!' Gramps cried. 'We've finished! I'm not sure why this ceiling is still coming down.' His eyes flicked upwards. 'These guys really need an emergency button or something.'

'Maybe when you're Father Christmas,' I said, 'you can make that a law?'

I figured he couldn't accuse me of getting my hopes up about him winning if we were about to be crushed flat. It was a shame. I really could picture him in the Santa outfit, hopping down chimneys . . .

That was it!

'The chimney!' I shouted. 'We forgot the chimney!'

Gramps grabbed two small rectangles of gingerbread. 'Quick! The icing!'

He held the pieces in place while I piped icing onto them. I then piped icing onto another two rectangles so we could make a long box. Heart pounding, I jammed the chimney on top of the house, and Gramps added a last little curl of icing like smoke.

CLUNK.

The ceiling stopped. Then, ever so slowly, it began to rise.

'We were seconds away from being as flat as gingerbread,' I said as we stared at the ceiling, panting.

'Saved by a chimney!' said Gramps.

As if in response, a red card shot out of the gingerbread house's chimney, smacking Gramps on the forehead.

'Ow!'

I caught the card and read it aloud: '*Climb down the flue to find your clue.*'

A moment passed.

'Does "flue" mean chimney?' I asked.

Gramps nodded.

We both looked at the chimney on the gingerbread house.

'You're joking,' said Gramps.

Another red card shot out of the chimney and hit me on the head this time.

I read it: '*Hurry up, won't you?*'

'Right,' said Gramps. 'In you go. I'll give you a boost.'

He cupped his hands and I stepped on his palms, then scrambled onto the table. I was leaning over the house . . . and then I found myself in the surprisingly wide and slightly sticky gingerbread chimney. It felt like I was falling down and up the chimney at exactly the same

time. I could hear that Gramps was right behind me by all his screaming.

'We're nearly there,' I yelled. 'I can see the li—'

I broke off as the chimney spat me out and I found myself rolling onto a snowy roof. I looked up at the starry night sky and the cool air on my skin was lovely compared to the heat of the kitchen we'd just been in. I scrambled to my feet and peered into the chimney, which was now made out of brick and not gingerbread, and saw that Gramps was a bit stuck. I reached in and yanked him out.

Gramps dusted himself down and I realised neither of us had our aprons on any more.

'That has got to be the weirdest thing that's ever happened to me.' Gramps sniffed his arm. 'And I really smell of gingerbread.'

I sniffed my arm too; Gramps was right. 'I guess there are worst things to smell of.'

'Is that another clue?' Gramps asked, pointing

to a red envelope stuck to the chimney with a gumdrop.

I opened it and then read it out loud:

'Some get toys and some get coal.
It all depends on self-control.
Santa checks not once but twice
Who's been naughty and who's been . . .'

'Nice!' we both shouted.

We high-fived, all chimney trauma forgotten. The Merrimans really are great at puzzles.

'Mikey,' Gramps said, squinting. 'What's that spinning above your head?'

I looked up. A shimmering holographic tablet hovered in the air. I reached for it, and the device became solid in my hands.

'It's Chief Elf's tablet,' I said, tapping the screen.

I saw immediately that it was showing Santa's

Naughty and Nice Lists. Names from all over the world scrolled past in two columns. This year, the Naughty List was much longer than the Nice one.

I handed the tablet to Gramps, who scowled as his eyes flicked over the names.

'Congratulations, Mikey and Curtis Merriman!' came a voice.

I jumped as Chief Elf stepped out from behind the chimney.

'Very well done,' he said, shaking both our hands. 'You are the first team to complete every room in the Clockmaker's Workshop, which is why you've been awarded the privilege of seeing the Naughty and Nice Lists. It's quite an honour to peek behind the curtain.'

'Yes!' I whooped, punching the air. We'd finally won a task! For the first time, I let myself hope that maybe Gramps *could* become the next Santa.

'Now, please hand over the tablet,' said Chief Elf, extending his hand.

Gramps hesitated. He quickly tapped something on the screen, then handed the tablet back. 'Here you go.'

Chief Elf let out a loud gasp.

'Curtis Merriman! What have you done with the Naughty and Nice Lists?!'

19

'**WHAT ARE YOU TALKING ABOUT?**'
I demanded.

Chief Elf shook the tablet at Gramps. 'The list
has disappeared! *Poof!* Gone!'

Gramps frowned. 'Huh? Let me see . . .' He
took the tablet from Chief Elf and peered at it.
'I'm so sorry. I must've pressed the wrong button.'
He shook his head regretfully. 'Grandfathers
should be kept from technology at all costs,
I always say.'

Oh no. How could Gramps make such a HUGE

mistake? He was excellent with technology! It must have been the excitement of winning the challenge that made his fingers slip.

I glanced at Gramps and noticed he had a very mischievous look on his face as he handed

it back to Chief Elf. *Oh, Gramps, what have you done?*

'Mr Merriman, you MUST tell me what you've done with the lists if you wish to remain part of Santa Search!' cried Chief Elf.

He tapped the tablet frantically and twisted it round, showing Gramps a blank page with an error icon that looked like a bin.

'Chief Elf,' I said quickly. 'Please don't kick Gramps out of Santa Search! If he deleted the list, I'm sure he is very sorry.'

'Extremely sorry,' Gramps said – though, suspiciously, he didn't sound sorry in the slightest.

'Is there a backup?' I asked quickly.

Chief Elf shook his head. 'Sugar Plum always said we should have one, but I never got round to it.' He blinked hard. 'Thousands of elf hours, months of espionage and the best spy training in the land – all WASTED!' Chief Elf pinched the bridge of his nose. 'I need a moment.'

He stomped away and went to sit on the edge of the roof.

Gramps sighed. 'Now before you start, Mikey, I don't regret doing it,' he said. 'No one is all good or all bad, especially not kids. You're still figuring out who you are!' He shrugged. 'There's naughty *and* nice in all of us.'

I couldn't believe what I was hearing! He'd done it on purpose?

'But, Gramps,' I said, 'what if we get booted out of the competition?'

'Mikey, I know you want me to be Father Christmas because you think it'll make me happier now that your gran's gone.' Gramps laid an arm over my shoulder. 'But the only thing I know for sure is that all kids deserve a bit of joy at Christmas – even if they happen to be more naughty than nice. That's the kind of Father Christmas I'd want to be, and if the Santa Search elves disagree with that . . .

well, then I wouldn't have been happy here anyway.'

I sighed. Gramps really was the best and it was very annoying.

The other teams took a while to gather on the roof of the Clockmaker's Workshop.

'Were you two first?' Ella asked, grinning at me and Gramps. 'Well done, Merrimans! Must be nice to be in Chief Elf's good books.'

'It was, but then there was a tiny mix-up with the tablet . . .' I replied weakly.

'Is that why Chief Elf looks like a storm cloud about to burst?' Lola Faith asked.

'It's gone . . . *Totally gone!*' Chief Elf was still pacing back and forth, muttering furiously.

'What's gone?' Jackson asked, coming over to us.

'I accidentally deleted the Naughty and Nice Lists,' Gramps explained.

Everyone apart from me and Gramps gasped.

'Well, that's hardly an accident, old chap!' Chad Buckles said bluntly. 'That's a Christmas *catastrophe*. And it's only fair and right that it affects your score.'

'That's not fair at all!' I said. 'We'd already completed the escape rooms before the lists disappeared.'

'Mikey's right,' said Ella. 'And, if you ask me, it shouldn't have been so easy to delete if it was so important.'

Lola Faith chuckled. 'You must admit this is a rather good Christmas miracle for the kids on the Naughty List. Perhaps it's for the best . . . In fact, should there even be Naughty or Nice Lists?'

'I assure you, Ms Diaz, there is nothing good or funny about this!' Chad insisted. 'The Merrimans

should not be allowed to win this challenge. Chief Elf, what is your decision?'

Chief Elf walked slowly over to us, looking from Chad to Gramps, then back down at the tablet again, as if trying to work out what to do.

Eventually, he let out a deep sigh and said, 'I'll share my final decision on the scores shortly, but first we need to find Tara and Mina Bakhshi. They should have finished by now.'

'I hope they didn't get smushed in that kitchen,' Ella commented.

'Unlikely,' Chief Elf replied. '*I think*,' he added under his breath, and then called out, 'To the workshop!'

We found Mina and Tara in their first room – except their parlour looked rather different. There were origami snowflakes, origami reindeer and origami stars everywhere. And even a huge origami Santa!

'Why are you still in here?' asked Jackson. 'You

do realise you were meant to move on to other rooms, right? Listen to the sound of that clock!'

Jackson was right. He was practically bellowing over the ticking.

Chief Elf hurried over to the clock, pressing a button to stop and silence it.

'Wait, so it's not a Christmas decorating task?' Mina asked, her eyes wide with surprise.

'No,' I said. 'Didn't you see the instructions?'

Mina and Tara shook their heads.

I pointed at their Christmas tree but saw that there was no sign of the instructions tag.

'Oh, there aren't any instructions,' I said with a frown. 'That's strange,'

'Strange or not, this is definitely not a Christmas decorating task,' Chief Elf said briskly, 'and because you've run out of time, you've failed the third Santa Search challenge.'

'Oh, Tara! Oh, Mina!' Lola Faith exclaimed. 'You definitely would have won if it was a Christmas decoration task. Look at all this wonderful origami! Did you make them out of the wrapping paper?'

'Too right – that's exactly what we did,' Tara said, her face proud.

Jackson sniggered a little, but stopped when Gramps gave him a stern glare.

Lola Faith was right, I thought. Tara and Mina had created a brilliant origami Christmas scene!

Tara slung an arm round Mina. 'I came here thinking I might end up being the next Santa. Honestly, my whole life I've been trying to work out what I'm actually good at. What I'm meant to do, you know. Reckon I've finally found it.' She pointed to all the neat little paper creations and picked up a star. 'Did you know my name means "star" in Persian? Anyway, I reckon we should start a family business. Paper engineers – what do you say, Mina? You can be my assistant!'

Mina's eyebrows shot up. 'Do I get to skip out on school, then?'

Tara laughed. 'Nice try! You've still gotta go to school! But you can pitch in on weekends. As long as you're on top of your homework.'

Mina grinned. 'All right, Mum – I'd be honoured to be your assistant.'

'Well, that's decided,' Tara said. 'I'm quitting the contest.'

'Tara, Mina – thank you for your honesty

and hard work,' said Chief Elf, bowing deeply. 'I believe you gave this process your very best, but as you're the team with the lowest score, I am sad that your time in Christmasland ends here. However, I've no doubt your origami business will be incredibly successful. Christmasland will be your first customer when you're ready.'

Ella and I blinked at each other. Was Chief Elf being . . . *nice*?

Chief Elf clapped his hands and looked at us all. 'Santa Search isn't just about us deciding who best suits the role of Santa – it's an opportunity for you all to decide what you really want.' He beamed at the Bakhshis. 'This is an outcome Santa will be very proud of.'

Tara and Mina gave us all a hug as we stood outside the workshop. We helped them load

up a sleigh with their origami art and then we were waving goodbye.

'Another one bites the dust,' said Jackson, grinning as Mina and Tara's sleigh disappeared. 'Only three teams left now!'

Chief Elf gave a little cough. 'The positions after the third challenge are as follows.' And, with a wave of his hand, the leader board appeared.

1ST
CHAD AND JACKSON BUCKLES

2ND
CURTIS AND MIKEY MERRIMAN

3RD
FAITH AND ELLA DIAZ

I grabbed Gramps's arm.
'Second place!' I whispered.

'Cooyah! Can't believe it!' Gramps said back, giving me a squeeze.

Did this mean Gramps actually had a chance at being Santa?

20

UNLIKE YESTERDAY, BREAKFAST WAS in the Decked Halls. It was quiet, and everyone seemed deep in thought. Jackson and Chad chose to sit far away from everyone else. They were probably thinking the same as me: *We were nearly there . . . Perhaps we could win this.*

Only Gramps seemed unaffected. He was humming 'This Christmas' and stacking his plate high with pancakes and waffles.

Back at the table, I sat across from Ella and cut into my waffles. They were piled with sliced bananas, blueberries, raspberries and a huge dollop of cream.

'Nice work, Mikey – that's the best waffle mountain I've ever seen,' said Ella as she drizzled melted chocolate over her cinnamon-sugar French toast. 'Don't you think yesterday felt like the *longest* day? I wonder how much time has passed outside Christmasland. Santa said time flows differently here, right?'

'Hopefully not too long – my parents were a bit worried about me missing school,' I said.

Ella giggled. 'My parents were as well, but Lola Faith can be very persuasive.'

'How are you feeling about today?' I asked.

'No nerves here. I'm already dressed for whatever is next. Besides, I know the best grandparent in Christmasland will win!' Ella nodded towards her lola, who was now chatting with Gramps.

'So you obviously mean Gramps,' I teased.

'Yeah, right. In your dreams!'

I nudged her. 'Obviously I want Gramps to win. But if it's not us, I hope it's you and Lola Faith.'

'Right back at you,' said Ella. And I knew she meant it.

Whatever happened next, whoever won this competition, I could tell I'd made a friend for life.

Suddenly Merry rushed in, waving a letter. 'I have an urgent message for Faith and Ella.'

Ella looked worried as she and Lola Faith ran over to Merry.

Had Ella done something wrong by mistake and broken the rules? Were they getting disqualified? I felt my stomach clench. Maybe it was guilt over the rules I had broken to get Gramps into this competition.

Lola Faith seemed every bit as anxious as Ella, and they held each other tightly. I could see that whatever Merry had to tell them was private,

so tried to focus on my breakfast as Merry spoke to the Diazes with a serious look on her face.

All of a sudden, Ella gave a shout of delight and punched the air. 'This is the BEST news ever!'

Lola Faith spun round to face me and Gramps. 'They've found a matching donor for Erwin. At last my grandson's kidney transplant can finally take place!'

'That *is* great news,' I said, breathing out a sigh of relief as I went over to Ella. 'When's the operation?'

'Today!' Ella replied. 'So me and Lola need to pack and leave right now. We want to be by his side when he wakes up from the operation.'

I nodded. I'd want to be there if something this big was happening to someone in my family. I hoped Mum and Dad got my message via Santa Mail that I sent before I went to bed yesterday.

Santa and the Sugar Plum Fairy entered the hall and took Lola Faith and Ella aside while Gramps and I finished our breakfast. I couldn't hear what was being said, but whatever it was had Ella and Lola Faith dabbing their eyes with

handkerchiefs passed to them by Sugar Plum. Santa gave them each a long hug before finding Merry to have a chat.

Ella came straight over to me and pulled me into a hug. I guess it was a morning for hugging.

'Apart from meeting Santa *and* flying to Christmasland,' she said, 'you've been the best part of this whole thing. I really wanted Lola to become the next Santa . . . but, more than that, I wanted my brother to get his transplant by Christmas.'

'It is my Christmas wish come true,' Lola Faith said, joining us. She looked at both me and Gramps. 'Please know I will never forget what you and Lolo Curtis did for us in the first challenge. You will both always be our heroes.'

'It was nothing,' said Gramps. 'It's been nice to make a new friend.'

My cheeks felt warm and I stared at the floor. 'I hope everything goes well with Erwin,'

I said, my throat catching. 'It's been . . . really good meeting and getting to know you.'

Lola Faith turned to Gramps. 'If it's not me who wins, then it had better be you,' she said. 'You're what Santa should be. And the way you and Mikey looked after us when you could've played to win – well, that says everything, doesn't it?'

She said it loud enough for everyone to hear. Including Santa. And definitely Chad and Jackson, who were still sitting far away. Their smug expressions had turned to outraged scowls.

'Don't let us keep you,' Chad called over, folding his arms. 'You've got a long trip ahead of you. Travel can be hard on the elderly.'

Ella rolled her eyes. She leaned in and whispered, 'Mikey Merriman, you'd better win this!'

With that, she turned away, linking arms with Lola Faith as they walked out of the hall.

Gramps gripped my shoulder as I let out a sad sigh.

'They'll be all right, Mikey Boy,' he said. 'Family's more important than any competition.'

I nodded and went back to the breakfast table, where Chad was talking to Sugar Plum. Jackson was now in the corner of the hall doing stretches, though I wasn't sure why. We didn't even know what the next and final challenge was yet – but, knowing Jackson and his dad, they probably had a pretty good idea.

Out of the corner of my eye, I noticed Sugar Plum slip something into Chad's coat pocket. Had it been a piece of paper?

I blinked.

When I looked again, they were just chatting like normal. Nothing suspicious. I shook my head. It had been a busy morning. Maybe I'd imagined it.

But then I heard Ella's voice in my head:

Be careful who you trust.

Perhaps we'd been right to think that someone had been sabotaging the challenges the whole time – but had we been wrong about who it was?

I wanted to tell Gramps what I'd seen, but Sugar Plum stood up and clapped loudly, smiling wide. In a burst of glitter, Chief Elf was by her side with his clipboard.

'Time for the final challenge,' Sugar Plum declared, her eyes sparkling. 'It's a test of stamina, planning, navigation *and* determination. Everything the next Santa will need. You'll be taking on a Santa Run . . . through Kringle Town.'

'What's Kringle Town?' Gramps asked, frowning.

Chief Elf opened his mouth to answer, but Jackson beat him to it.

'It's a replica town,' he said smoothly, 'just east of here, on the edge of Christmasland.'

I noticed Chief Elf scribbling something on his clipboard. Probably another tick for Jackson and his dad, or a comment saying how awesome they were.

'Thank you, Jackson,' said Sugar Plum. 'Correct as always. But the best way to know Kringle Town is to see it. Let's go!'

21

IT FELT SO STRANGE NOW THAT THERE WERE
only two teams left. Me and Gramps versus
Chad and Jackson.

We walked alongside Santa as we headed to
Kringle Town, but Gramps seemed lost in his own
world. I wondered what he was thinking about.

I adjusted the backpack on my shoulder,
which I'd run back to get before we left. I wanted
to make sure we had Gran-Angel with us as our
good-luck charm for this last challenge.

I cast a sideways glance at Santa, who looked

as if he had a lot on his mind. He always tried to act jolly and fun, but I could see the tiredness around his eyes. I think this competition to find his replacement had been hard on him as well as the Hopefuls.

Chad and Jackson had fallen slightly behind and were whispering to each other. What were they up to? Was Sugar Plum trying to sabotage them, or was she helping them to cheat? Either could be true.

Maybe I should just tell Santa? It was a big thing to accuse someone of cheating or sabotage, but I could mention what I saw at breakfast. I bit the side of my thumb and rehearsed what I wanted to say over and over in my head. But, when I finally opened my mouth, Jackson appeared out of nowhere and slid in between me and Santa.

'Santa, I've been meaning to ask,' Jackson said. 'During the winter of 1978, how did you manage to get through that snowstorm?'

Santa blinked. 'I'm surprised you know about that – it was well before your time.'

'I've been studying the Christmasland archives,' Jackson said. 'I think any serious candidate should.'

'Well, yes,' Santa said, nodding thoughtfully. 'That was Storm Winston. Wind, hail, snow, you name it. I remember it well. That year I decided to take the wild reindeer out as they're better in a big storm. Heavier coats and stronger as well. They didn't enjoy the weather, but they handled it brilliantly. Strong spirits, those ones.'

'Smart decision to try something different,' said Chad.

Santa smiled. 'That's what I'm hoping for with this Santa Search. Opening up the process – doing away with the idea that Santa has to act or look a certain way. It's the heart and smarts that matters. The next Santa has to be able to think clearly when things go sideways.'

I saw Santa glance at Gramps and smile. I felt my heart lurch – Santa wanted Gramps to be the next Father Christmas, I was sure of it.

'I imagine the year 2000 must've been a particularly challenging time,' said Chad, his voice full of polite admiration. 'All that digital uncertainty.'

Santa raised an eyebrow. 'Oh, don't remind me of the Millenium Bug. It was real, you know. Nasty little thing. Nearly scrambled the entire sleigh-routing system. But we got through it.'

I dropped back a few steps. I wanted to talk to Santa properly, but not with Chad and Jackson lurking either side of him. Gramps looked over at me and gave me a thumbs up.

'You good, Mikey?' he asked, slowing down to walk with me.

'I'm good, Gramps,' I replied.

I'm not sure why I hadn't told him about what I'd seen at breakfast. I think I was worried Gramps

would say we should walk away, if he thought the competition was rigged. Gramps hated cheats.

By the time we reached Kringle Town Square, Chief Elf was already waiting and he didn't waste any time.

'Kringle Town is made up of two tracks,' he told us. 'Each team will be assigned one route. Your job is simple: deliver every present in your sleigh to the correct home. First team back wins.'

Chad and Jackson immediately started whispering to each other again, and Chief Elf gave them a glare that settled them into silence before continuing.

'But, of course, nothing is ever quite that straightforward,' Chief Elf said. 'You'll face a few hazards along the way. Tripwires. Barking dogs. Sleeping elves.'

I raised a hand. 'Why are sleeping elves a hazard?'

'Because if you wake one, you get a time penalty,' he replied crisply.

Kringle Town was set in a valley, and I'd taken a good look at it as we'd approached. It had cobbled lanes, icy pavements and buildings of every shape and size. As well as log cabins and fairy-tale cottages, there were tower blocks with pretty fairy lights, bungalows with evergreen hedges and inflatable snowmen in the garden, and even a row of semi-detached brick houses with wheelie bins out front that looked a bit like my house.

'I'm guessing this is where Santa practises,' Gramps murmured beside me. 'All the types of homes he has to deliver to. Makes sense, doesn't it?'

It did. And it made the challenge ahead feel even more real.

Chief Elf squinted up at the sky, and we all watched as two enormous sleighs descended and landed in the centre of the square. One of the sleighs was blue and silver, sleek and gleaming. The other was red and gold, with velvet trim and polished brass runners. Both were loaded with neatly wrapped parcels and presents.

'Gramps. Look,' I said, pointing to the blue-and-silver sleigh. 'It's Aurora and Tempest.'

The reindeer gave a whinny of greeting and turned to face us.

'Can we take that sleigh?' I asked quickly. 'We've worked with those two reindeer. We know how they fly.'

Chief Elf gave a firm shake of his head. 'I'm afraid that sleighs have already been allocated.'

Before I could respond, Chad jumped in with a wide smile. 'Chief Elf, we don't mind swapping. We're not picky.'

Jackson chimed in. 'Happy to take whichever – we'd hate to ever be a problem.'

'Noted. It's important to know that the next Santa must be comfortable with all the reindeer,' said Santa.

His tone was gentle, but I still felt the sting. It wasn't a telling-off, but it was a reminder. This wasn't about comfort zones.

I swallowed and nodded. 'Understood.'

Gramps gave my arm a quiet squeeze.

We went over to our new reindeer and I really wished I had some sugar snap peas for them. It felt like a long time ago that we were talking to Sugar Plum and she was giving us advice on reindeer, but it had only been yesterday.

Chief Elf came over. 'Mikey and Curtis, meet Twinkle and Blazen.'

The two reindeer dipped their head in greeting. They had a different energy to Aurora and Tempest. Quieter and a bit more serious.

We clambered into the red-and-gold sleigh. Once we were settled, our reindeer trotted to the beginning of the track.

'You ready for this? Our final challenge,' Gramps asked.

'Born ready,' I said. Whatever happened next, I'd loved being in Christmasland with Gramps.

'I can't believe how far we've come,' Gramps said. 'Claudette would have loved this adventure.'

I hesitated, but then said softly, 'Well, Gramps, she's been with us the whole time. She deserves a proper view.'

I reached into my backpack and pulled out Gran-Angel.

Gramps took her in his hands and looked down at the little figure he'd carved by hand.

'Oh, Mikey.' For a moment, he didn't say anything more and I held my breath. Then he gave a slow nod and gently fixed Gran-Angel to the dashboard.

'There she is. Watching over us. Watching out for us.' Gramps smiled. 'Thank you for bringing her, Mikey. Let's do her proud.'

'Contenders, are you ready?' Sugar Plum called out.

She stood at the start line with a candy-striped flag. The fairy-elf's voice was sharp and she looked really tense, not smiley at all. It was as if I was seeing her properly for the first time and I realised that I absolutely needed to tell Gramps about her putting something in Chad's coat pocket. But there was no time. The race was about to start.

Sugar Plum raised her candy-striped flag. 'On your marks . . . Get set . . . go, go, go!'

The flag dropped.

The sky went completely dark.

It was suddenly night-time.

22

I WAS KNEE-DEEP IN PRESENTS, READING THE labels by torchlight and sorting them into piles by street name. I still couldn't get over the fact they'd made it night-time in Kringle Town for the final challenge. It definitely made things trickier.

What really blew my mind, though, was that every single present had writing on it that described the gift as well as the name and address of who it was for. Our manual in the sleigh told us that the ink was only visible to those from or in Christmasland!

Up front, Gramps had a map and he guided us to our first destination. The sleigh banked left towards Bauble Boulevard.

Presents for Mistletoe Avenue went in one corner of the sleigh. Presents for Carroll Road went in another. The pile for Bauble Boulevard was all ready to go. Gramps and I didn't talk much – there wasn't time for that. We were in a race!

The view over the edge of the sleigh was breathtaking. Lights twinkled below and smoke puffed out of chimneys – little breaths on the air from sleeping houses.

'Imagine what it must feel like to do this for real,' Gramps said. 'Children wait all year for Christmas Eve. How amazing it must be to bring them the gifts they've been wishing for.' He gently pulled on the reins. 'We're almost there, Mikey. The first house!'

The sleigh suddenly leaned to the left and a tearing sound came from near the front. The

reindeer pawed the air, trying to keep us straight.

'What's going on?' I asked, gripping the edge of the sleigh. 'That doesn't sound good.'

Gramps was already tightening the reins, his jaw set. 'I think there's something wrong with one of the straps attaching the reindeer to the sleigh. We need to land quickly before it goes completely.'

The sleigh tilted again, this time worse. Gramps lowered us in a tight arc. We dipped over the rooftops and touched down in a garden in a flurry of snow, skidding slightly before settling. Not smooth, but safe.

Gramps was out of his seat in seconds, crunching across the snow. I followed, scanning the sleigh with my torch.

'Here,' I called, kneeling near the front. 'The strap attached to the reindeer's neck harness is tearing. Look – the leather's already split almost halfway through.'

Gramps unwound his scarf and began knotting it into place with quick, firm movements.

'Will it hold?' I asked.

'Your gran knitted this – it'll hold, but we've got to move fast and get through these deliveries.'

He checked and double-checked the knot, pulling it hard. The leather harness gave a low creak in response.

'Back in,' Gramps said. 'We've got a race to win.'

The sleigh lifted slowly but was perfectly balanced. I kept my eyes fixed on the knotted scarf as we rose. Soon the reindeer found their rhythm again, and we headed for our first address on Bauble Boulevard. Time to get delivering.

Sometimes Gramps climbed down the chimneys while I passed the presents to him from above. At other houses, when his arms were too full, we both squeezed down together.

For homes without chimneys, we used the special kit tucked inside the sleigh, next to the

manual. It was a set of small wooden panels, a bit like the gingerbread sheets we'd used in the Clockmaker's Workshop. With a dab of glue and a touch of Christmas magic, we could build a chimney in seconds.

Honestly, nothing can beat Christmas magic.

The best part – besides leaving gifts for sleeping children that were in fact sleeping elves – were the mince pies and cookies. Gramps always ate one and brought another back for me. They were all delicious and it seemed impossible to get full on them. I'll say it again – Christmas magic is awesome!

We were zooming through the deliveries, avoiding every trap that Chief Elf had hidden. The tripwires didn't catch us. The mechanical dogs didn't slow us down. But then we reached a house with a chimney frozen solid.

Gramps peered into it. 'Chuh! No way we're getting down there.'

Behind us, Twinkle and Blazen huffed impatiently, clouds of steam curling from their nostrils as they stamped the snow on the icy rooftop.

I chuckled at their snorting – I'd been right that Twinkle and Blazen were more serious than

Aurora and Tempest. They were also *way* more competitive.

An idea popped into my head.

'Twinkle, Blazen, over here,' I said, guiding the reindeer towards the bricks of the chimney. 'Do your huffing on these. Nice and warm, please.'

The two reindeer stepped closer, snorting furiously, and long streams of warm breath hit the icy bricks. The snow clinging to the chimney began to melt. A few more breaths and we heard the ice inside the chimney crack and slide downwards.

Gramps looked down the chimney. Perfect.

'That's a big enough gap,' he said, and wasted no time wriggling down as if he'd been doing this Father Christmas job for years. In some ways he had been, I guess.

When Gramps climbed back up, he was dusty with soot, and had to shake icy shards off his clothes.

'Slippery work, but someone's got to do it,' he said, grinning at me.

And on we went . . .

At 42 Present Crescent, I joined him down the chimney and met a really excited caramel-coloured poodle.

I managed to keep it quiet by singing a little lullaby and rubbing its tummy while Gramps filled the stockings and arranged the presents beneath the tree.

Back in the sleigh, flying towards North Star Lane, I glanced at the opposite track and spotted Chad and Jackson on a rooftop. Their sleigh was almost completely empty of presents. I felt a weight settle in my stomach. How were they delivering so quickly to the homes?

It was dark, but in the moonlight I could make out their silhouettes and reindeer – and then I realised something. Chad and Jackson were not alone.

'Gramps!' I said urgently. 'We need to park the sleigh. It's important.'

'How important?' he asked.

'*Really* important. The FUTURE OF CHRISTMAS *important*!'

23

GRAMPS DIDN'T ASK ANY MORE QUESTIONS and landed the sleigh on the nearest roof. I jumped out and began tearing through the presents.

'Mikey,' Gramps said, frowning. 'You can't open someone else's gift!'

'I'm borrowing it. Just for a second.'

Finally, I found what I was searching for: a long, slim box wrapped in blue paper with silver stars. I peeled it open and lifted out a telescope.

Gramps helped me screw the pieces together, then I raised it to my eye . . . and saw exactly what I hoped I wouldn't.

'Look,' I said, handing it to Gramps.

Through the telescope, he saw what I had seen. Sugar Plum. On the Buckles' sleigh. Passing them gifts. The third member of their team.

'They're cheating.' Gramps sounded furious. 'But what takes place in the dark will come out in the light.'

'We need to tell Santa,' I said. 'Right now.'

Gramps didn't hesitate. We turned the sleigh round and raced back to find Santa.

We spotted him at the finish line.

'Chad and Jackson are cheating.' The words were out of my mouth before the sleigh had even fully stopped beside him. 'And Sugar Plum is helping!'

'It's true,' said Gramps.

He jumped down from the sleigh and passed

the telescope to Santa. Gramps pointed towards the house on North Star Lane. 'Over there.'

Gramps and I waited quietly while Santa peered through the lens. After a few seconds, he lowered the telescope.

'I see,' said Santa. 'I see all too clearly.'

His shoulders sagged with disappointment, and I felt incredibly sad for him. He was like a balloon that had lost all its air. Not only had Santa been betrayed by Chad and Jackson – but, worse, he'd been betrayed by Sugar Plum.

'What's wrong?' Chief Elf asked, rushing up to us, his face full of concern. 'Santa, are you feeling all right? Do you feel unwell? Why are these two back already with a sleigh still full of presents?'

'Chad and Jackson are cheating,' Santa said with a heavy sigh. 'And Sugar Plum is helping them.'

Chief Elf put a hand on Santa's arm. 'Don't despair. We'll deal with these cheats and then figure out the next step. It will be OK, Santa.'

Chief Elf looked as sad as Santa, and I knew instantly he had nothing to do with any cheating. I had totally misread him. He might have been stern but he was definitely not a cheat.

All four of us crowded together into the red sleigh. Both Santa and Gramps went to pick up the reins, then shared an awkward chuckle.

'I would be honoured to ride in your sleigh, Curtis Merriman,' Santa said, smiling.

'Let's catch those cheats,' said Gramps, and in a blink Twinkle and Blazen were soaring up into the sky.

Chief Elf and I took turns with the telescope to keep everyone updated on Chad, Jackson and Sugar Plum, who had just landed on the rooftop of a long, low building.

'It looks like they've got *two* maps,' I said.

'Hold tight. We'll get to the bottom of this very soon,' Gramps said as Twinkle and Blazen raced through the air.

We landed on the far end of the long rooftop. At the other end, Jackson and his dad were in their sleigh checking a sheet of paper, with Sugar Plum peering over Jackson's shoulder. Gramps had touched down so quietly and smoothly that they hadn't even heard us.

'Hey, you cheaters!' I cried the moment I reached them.

Sugar Plum jumped in surprise, but Jackson gave me a glare that said, *Shove off!*

'Care to explain what's going on?' said Santa coldly as he joined me.

Jackson gave a squeak of surprise and dropped the piece of paper. I snatched it up quickly and read it before showing it to Chief Elf and Santa.

It was a hand-drawn map with all the tripwires and sleeping elves and other traps marked on it. It even had shortcuts. That explained why the Buckles had been so quick!

Chief Elf stared at the map. 'This is definitely

Sugar Plum's handwriting. As Santa said, would any of you care to explain?'

Chad, Jackson and Sugar Plum glanced at one another in guilty silence.

'Fine, I'll speak,' I said. 'I don't think this is the first time she's helped them. I think she's been sabotaging the rest of the Hopefuls and Helpers from the beginning.'

Sugar Plum scowled at me, but I took a deep breath and carried on.

'In the first task, some of the maps weren't working properly. I think they had been tampered with,' I said.

Sugar Plum wouldn't meet my eye, but she kept an innocent look on her face.

'And then the reindeer challenge . . .' I went on. 'It never really made sense to me that Chad and Jackson's reindeer seemed so tame from the start – Sugar Plum must've made sure of that. And how about the reindeer that fell asleep,

which disqualified Mina and Tara? Sugar Plum told us that sweet food gives reindeer a sugar crash, but I remember that she was the one who gave them the cookie for the reindeer.'

Sugar Plum was definitely squirming now. Her wings were fluttering anxiously.

'And just now our harness almost snapped in mid-air. I'm sure the tear in the leather was deliberate.'

'Mikey, if you had these concerns, why didn't you say anything?' Gramps asked. 'You know you can tell me anything.'

I felt my cheeks grow warm. I *should* have said something. And I knew there was still so much I had to tell Gramps about how we got into this competition in the first place, but not right now.

'I had suspicions,' I admitted, 'but it's only today that things have started slotting into place.'

Santa looked stunned. 'How could I have missed this?'

Chad scoffed. 'If you ask me, Mikey's making things up. A tired mind can invent things. All this is just too much for him.'

'Yeah, you ought to rein him in, *Gramps*,' sneered Jackson.

'I'm not making any of this up,' I said calmly. 'And you know it, *Jackson*.'

Gramps put his hand on my shoulder. 'I believe Mikey. Unlike you lot, he's not a liar.' His eyes met Jackson's and he shook his head. 'This whole time I thought you and your dad knew everything about Christmasland and that's why you were winning, but now I see it was never about *what* you knew – it was about *who* you knew! *Sugar Plum*.'

'You're a disgrace to elfkind, Sugar Plum,' Chief Elf said. 'Why did you do it?'

Sugar Plum narrowed her eyes at Chief Elf.

'Fine. I admit it. I agreed to give them a little help,' the fairy-elf confessed. 'And I'd do it again.'

Sugar Plum squared her shoulders, her wings now still. 'You all think Christmas runs on candy canes and good tidings. But I know the truth. The elves are the engine of this place. We work through the night when it counts. We make the gifts and

we fix the sleigh. But when the Christmas lights go up and the Christmas songs play, it's always *Santa this* and *Santa that*. No one writes songs about us.' Sugar Plum's hands clenched into fists. 'I've given everything to Christmas over the years. But things never change. Or so I thought. I was full of hope when Santa said he was retiring, but it didn't even *occur* to him to ask an elf to take his place.'

'B-but the old magic says Santa must be a human,' Santa spluttered, clearly shocked by Sugar Plum's words.

'Of course it does,' Sugar Plum said. 'Why would the old magic ever think an elf would be up to the job?' She let out a deep sigh. 'So yes – when Buckles Enterprises came calling with ideas for innovating the Christmas experience, I listened to them, because *they* listened to *me*.'

She turned to Santa. 'I didn't want to mess up Christmas. I just wanted to be heard. I helped

them cheat because I thought that, maybe, if they were the winners, then for once someone would take the elves seriously.' She glanced at me guiltily. 'I never meant for Faith and Ella's sleigh to get caught in the Ice Cliffs. I fiddled a few maps to slow people down, not to put them in danger. And the fraying on your sleigh harness, Mikey – I swear, it wasn't supposed to be dangerous. Only enough to delay you. I didn't know it would almost snap while you were flying.'

I frowned. It sounded like Sugar Plum was telling the truth, but I had to be sure.

'Did you mess with the snowflake carriage too? Back in Liverpool? Is that why ours nearly fell off?'

Sugar Plum shook her head, a flicker of surprise in her eyes. 'No. That wasn't me. Just some rushed handiwork from the set-up crew we worked with because we were outside Christmasland. Not elf built. Elves get it right.'

'Elves do get it right,' Chief Elf said. 'So I

can't understand how you got things so wrong, Sugar Plum.' Chief Elf sounded more sad than angry. 'You say that Santa gets all the credit and that the elves do all the work, but you've never really appreciated what Santa does. You've never watched his despair that he can't get a gift to every child because they're on the Naughty List. You've never sat with him as he reads a thousand letters from children who've lost too much to wish for presents. Or the pain it causes him when a child wishes for a person who's gone and can't be brought back.'

Sugar Plum's shoulders dropped. 'I don't regret wanting more. But I regret my actions. I really do.' She looked at Chief Elf and Santa. 'I know now that I can't stay here in Christmasland any longer. I need to do something different.'

'That is your choice, Sugar Plum,' Santa said softly. 'But we're here if you ever want to come back.'

'Thank you, and I'm sorry,' Sugar Plum whispered. 'I'll miss you, Santa.'

Chief Elf scowled at Chad and Jackson. 'You two, on the other hand, have no choice. You are disqualified. Time for you to leave.'

⭐⭐⭐⭐⭐

'I can't believe it was them all along,' I said, shaking my head as Sugar Plum, Chad and Jackson left Kringle Town Square to get their things from the lodges in the main village.

Chad and Jackson had not seemed at all sorry for the cheating, but they did seem excited that Sugar Plum had agreed to be their new Vice President of Operations.

'They're welcome to each other,' Gramps said. 'I just hope Sugar Plum finds what she is looking for. I'm not sure how it is going to go, working with those two cheaters.'

I looked up at Gramps. 'It's only us left,' I said. 'Out of six pairs, we're the last ones in Santa Search.'

Gramps chuckled. The scarf Gran had knitted for him was back around his neck and flapping in the breeze. 'I'd noticed, Mikey Boy,' he replied.

'So you know what that means?' I breathed. 'You won! *You* are the next Father Christmas!'

A flood of emotions crossed Gramps's face at the same time. Excitement. Fear. Disbelief. Doubt. And something else . . .

'I am so proud of what we achieved,' Gramps said. 'Saving Ella and Faith, flying on a wild reindeer, solving puzzles, making a gingerbread house under pressure, and magic chimneys . . . Every one of those things makes me feel like a champion because I did them with you.' Gramps swallowed hard. 'I came here not knowing if this competition – this job – was really for me. I came here not knowing who I was without my

darling Claudette.' He looked down at Gran-Angel, which he'd taken from the sleigh. 'But, after all we've been through, I know I am strong enough to do this job. Good enough to do this job. As long as Santa actually wants me to take over, and it's not simply because no one else is left.'

Chad, Jackson and Sugar Plum trudged back to the square, carrying their luggage.

Jackson scowled at us as he got into a sleigh that was to take him home, but I ignored him. They had caused so much trouble for us at every step of this competition, but soon they'd be gone and Christmasland would be getting the new Santa it deserved!

Chad wore a strange look on his face as he glanced over at Gramps. It made me feel uneasy.

Chad approached the sleigh but, instead of getting in, he turned round, then announced, 'Santa and Chief Elf, before I leave, I have some

information to share with you all.'

I could hear my heartbeat pounding in my ears. Why did Jackson have a smug smirk on his face? Why did Sugar Plum look like she was feeling sorry for me?

'What is it?' Santa asked. 'Is it important?'

'Yes, indeed it is,' Chad said smoothly. 'Very important, especially for Curtis Merriman, who I'm sure isn't aware that his grandson broke the rules too. It seems that we're not the only cheats here.'

I stiffened, as if someone had shoved snow down my back.

'Yuh dare call my grandson a cheat!' Gramps's voice was the most serious I had ever heard it. His slight Jamaican accent, which always added warmth to his words, suddenly sounded much sharper.

I put a hand on his arm. Words bubbled up my throat, but they wouldn't leave my mouth.

'Chad Buckles, if you are going to make an allegation of cheating, you'd better be able to back it up. What rules exactly were broken?' Chief Elf asked sceptically.

'Well, to start, Mikey submitted old footage of his grandfather in the application. The rules were very clear that the footage must be recent,' said Chad, raising an eyebrow at me.

Everyone turned in my direction – Santa, Chief Elf, Gramps, Chad, Jackson, Sugar Plum.

'How did you find out?' I asked quietly.

Gramps took a sharp intake of breath, realising I'd pretty much admitted my guilt. I couldn't meet his eyes, although I felt his gaze on me.

Chad pulled out a memory stick, which he handed to Santa.

'Here's the proof. It's all on there. Sugar Plum shared all the successful applications for Santa Search with me, so I could study the competition

when we arrived in Christmasland. Once I had the videos, I also got my team back at Buckle Enterprises in London to do a deep dive. It was my people who rumbled Beatrice Bolt's disguise, and Sugar Plum let Chief Elf and Santa know about Beatrice's plan for a news story. My people even got her editor to leak the Christmasland piece early and not wait until she was back.'

Chad smirked, then he looked right at me. 'As well as that . . . my team figured out that the footage you entered was definitely more than a year old,' he said. 'As an entrepreneur who supports ingenuity and risk-taking, I have

to say, Mikey, that I did rather admire your effort and . . . erm, creativity – shall we call it?'

'Mikey? Is he telling the truth?' Gramps asked softly. His eyes were wide behind his glasses. 'Whatever you tell me, I'll believe you. I'm sure Chad and his team wouldn't be above making up stories to frame you.'

I raised my eyes to meet his. I knew he'd believe me if I said that Chad was lying. But I was ready to come clean. This secret had been a heavy one to carry even in all our moments of excitement and joy in Christmasland. In a strange way, a part of me was relieved the truth was out. But it didn't stop me being terrified of what Gramps would think of me.

24

'**I**T'S THE TRUTH,' I SAID MISERABLY. 'I ENTERED you into the competition without your permission or knowledge – that was against the rules as well.' I covered my face with my hands. 'I'm so sorry, Gramps. I only did it because I wanted to make you happy again. I thought getting you to come here would bring the old Gramps back. That was my wish. But I don't want old Gramps.' I wiped a tear away. 'Because I understand now that losing Gran changed you – it changed all of us – that's OK.' I sniffed as

I realised something in that moment. 'You'll always be my Other Father Christmas, with or without the community grotto. I love you, Gramps.'

'Oh, Mikey Boy.' Gramps put down Gran-Angel and pulled me into the biggest hug ever, and I gave a shuddering sob. 'I love you too. You made a mistake but our mistakes don't define us.'

Chad coughed. 'Mistakes might not define you,' he said, 'but do they get you disqualified?'

'If we have to go, they should go as well,' Jackson added stubbornly.

I glanced over as Santa clicked his fingers and the sleigh rose into the air with a jolt.

'What happens next is no concern of yours, Mr Buckles,' Santa said. 'I've been asking myself this for a while, but how in all of Christmasland did you even get through the selection process?'

Sugar Plum looked sheepish. 'I may have helped them with that. I interfered with the

shortlisting program, but you did say yes to the Buckles as well, Santa.'

'You interfered with my shortlisting program!' Chief Elf gaped in surprise at her. 'Impossible! I built that myself.'

'I've always been better at building than you thought.' Sugar Plum sounded sad and defiant all at the same time. 'But you never let me help. I'll be seeing you around.'

Santa nodded. 'Time for the three of you to go . . . Ho ho ho!' he boomed, and the sleigh took off at super speed.

The Buckles' screams of terror were soon just an echo.

Santa came over and placed a hand on Gramps's shoulder. 'I know you weren't part of this, Curtis, but it was your responsibility to read the contract before you signed it.' Santa sighed. 'You are now disqualified and will be sent home immediately. I'm so very sorry it's come to this.'

'Now, Santa – wait,' said Chief Elf, rushing forward. 'Mikey was wrong to break the rules, no question. But he's a child. And from where I'm standing, his intentions seem a lot purer than Chad Buckles' desire to be Santa.' He paused and glanced at Gramps. 'And Curtis was completely innocent in all of this. It would feel rather harsh to punish him for something he didn't mean to do.' Chief Elf clasped his hands behind his back. 'The decision is yours, Santa . . . but I think Curtis Merriman would make a very fine Santa Claus indeed.'

I blinked in surprise. I would never have imagined that Chief Elf of all people would have argued our case – especially after Gramps deleted the Naughty and Nice Lists! I'd misjudged him. Just like I'd misjudged a lot of things.

'But it is not my decision,' Santa said wearily. 'The old magic has rules, Chief Elf. You know this. The Santa Search rules are rooted in magic.

The new Santa must have followed the rules for the contest. We're out of options.'

'But if there's no new Santa . . . what happens now?' I asked.

Santa rubbed at his beard, and suddenly he looked ancient. Appearing silently, two elves brought a stool and he lowered himself onto it slowly.

'The truth is,' he said, 'my Christmas magic has been running low for a long time. I've had enough to keep things ticking along. But this search for my successor . . .' He pressed his hands together and stared down at the ground. 'Running the Santa Search, opening the portal for you all, holding everything together during the tasks . . . it drained the last of my Christmas powers. I'm pretty much running on empty.' He shrugged, then sighed. 'The time difference between Christmasland and everywhere else has been especially inside out and upside down.'

I shared a look with Gramps. This whole time, we thought Santa was retiring because he was ready for a change, not because he had run out of magic.

Santa gave a faint, tired smile. 'I was a fool to leave things so late. I should have started searching for my replacement years ago, but I wasn't ready to give up the best job ever.' He glanced up at us. 'I thought by now there would be the perfect candidate. A new Santa, full of new magic, ready to take over just in time for Christmas Eve. That's how it was meant to work. But there's no one left in the running. And without a Santa . . . the Christmas magic won't regenerate and be passed on.'

'Are you cancelling Christmas?' Gramps gasped.

'No,' Santa said quickly. 'Not *cancelling*. Christmas is not only about Santa. But there'll be no deliveries. No sleigh rides. No stocking surprises. That part of Christmas is . . . on pause.

Until we can figure out whether Santa still has a place in the world.'

'You can't mean that,' I said. 'You're just tired. That's all.'

'It's more than tiredness, Mikey. The magic is almost all gone. Maybe this is a sign that Santa should be retired for good.'

25

SNOWFLAKES WERE GENTLY FALLING BY
the time Gramps and I got out of the sleigh
outside our house in Toxteth. Gramps had barely
said a word since we left Christmasland, and I
grew more worried the longer he was quiet.

He unlocked our front door and we walked in.
I never thought I'd ever say this, but it didn't feel
so good to be back home. Not like this.

I had imagined our grand return to Toxteth
as champions, with news of our win reaching our
neighbours, friends and family. Instead, all we

had to share now was the story of how I messed everything up by breaking the rules.

The house was super quiet, which made Gramps's silence even louder. I followed him into the kitchen. He rummaged through the cupboards and took out a grater and milk pan, followed by a cocoa stick, nutmeg and cinnamon.

'There might not be hot chocolate flowing from the taps, but I can still make a pretty mean cocoa tea if you'd like?' Gramps said kindly as he took the milk out of the fridge.

Tears pricked my eyes at the softness in his voice. He was being so nice and trying to make me feel better when I was the one who had ruined everything – not just for Gramps but for everyone.

'I'm so sorry, Gramps,' I said, blinking my tears away.

'I don't want to hear any more *sorry*s,' Gramps said. He stopped grating the cocoa stick and gave

me a hug. 'We all make mistakes. What's done is done.'

He went over to the cooker to heat the milk.

'It didn't turn out exactly like you'd hoped, Mikey Boy, but you did help me rediscover my love of Christmas. If it wasn't for you, I'd still be too sad and angry at the thought of celebrating Christmas without your gran to enjoy it.'

'So you're not angry at me for not telling you I'd broken the rules?' I asked.

Gramps shook his head. 'Of course not, Mikey. It wasn't the right thing to do, but I understand why you did it, and it means the world to me how much you cared. Between you and me, I wouldn't change a thing about our Christmasland adventure.'

Maybe Gramps could forgive me, but I didn't know if I could forgive myself. I sniffed and squeezed my eyes, trying to stop the tears again. When I opened them . . . there in front of me

were Mum and Dad dressed as Mr and Mrs Claus!

'Mikey! Dad!' said my parents at the same time, and we had the best family hug ever.

'Why are you dressed like that?' I asked after we unwrapped ourselves.

'Your mum and I decided to keep the grotto going in Gramps's absence. It's been brilliant. We totally love it – even if we do have big shoes to fill.'

Mum peered at Gramps. 'Hang on, we heard on the news that you were the last Hopeful. Does that mean you're the new Santa? It's the twenty-third of December – surely you should be getting ready in Christmasland?'

Gramps added some more milk to the pan. 'I'll tell you everything, but let's do it over some cocoa tea.'

Mum and Dad went to get changed, and I headed to my room. I noticed a pile of homework on my desk – I was going to be busy over the

Christmas break! Then I spotted that the poster for Santa Search was still there too, next to the homework. I gazed at it, my eyes tracing the words. Seeing this poster dance in the air felt like so long ago. I folded it neatly, then tucked it into my pocket and went downstairs to the front room where a cup of cocoa tea was waiting for me. Meanwhile, Gramps was trying to answer the flurry of questions that Mum and Dad were firing at him.

'What's Santa like in real life?'

'Did you meet Rudolph?'

'Was Christmasland like what we saw on TV?'

'Who was your favourite elf?'

Gramps didn't seem to mind. He leaned back in his chair, eyes bright, sipping cocoa tea between his answers.

OK, so things hadn't gone the way I'd hoped, but he seemed different somehow. It wasn't that he was over his grief about Gran. It sat there still

with him, but I could see the other parts of him as well. Something had shifted for him.

The competition, the challenges, the friends we'd made, the chaos with Chad and Jackson and, of course, the disqualification. It was hard to believe it had all happened in just a few days, but it had been nearly three weeks in normal time. I guessed this was what Santa had meant about the time difference between Christmasland and here being inside out and upside down.

Mum and Dad had agreed with Gramps about me breaking the rules. They said it was wrong, but they understood why I'd done it. While Gramps kept the stories going, I slipped outside to get some air.

The garden was quiet. Snow had settled over everything, soft and thick. I zipped up my coat and lay on the ground, letting my arms and legs press into the snow. I moved my arms up and down, and my legs from side to side, making a snow angel.

The sky above was still and dark. No colour trails. No magical shimmer like the sky in Christmasland. Only the ordinary night sky. I stared at it anyway, because it was still beautiful.

I couldn't stop thinking about what Santa had said. About his magic running out. About not knowing whether there would even be a Santa in the future. I still couldn't decide what was worse: Santa not being able to deliver presents? Or the question of whether Santa was needed at all?

The image of Santa's face, when he'd said all that, stuck with me. He hadn't looked upset. Just emptied out. I wished there was a way I could fix it.

Suddenly something flickered in the sky.

I sat up. A thin band of green light was stretching across the moonlit clouds. Another shimmer. A pulse of pale blue. The Northern Lights swirling! Faint at first, then stronger, like they were gathering in one place.

I stood up and brushed snow off myself, my gaze fixed on the sky.

Then a shape broke through the colour. A sleigh. Red and gold. Pulled by reindeer.

There was no mistaking it.

It was him.

26

SANTA SWOOPED DOWN UNTIL THE SLEIGH
and reindeer hovered just above my head.
Then, very slowly, they landed with a soft thud
next to my snow angel.

I could tell my mouth was hanging open
because I could see my breath on the cold night
air. Santa was *here* – in my garden, in Toxteth,
with his sleigh and reindeer who were patiently
waiting!

'Good evening, Mikey,' Santa said, getting
down from the sleigh. 'I can tell by the look on

your face I'm the last person you thought you'd see tonight, but you and your grandfather left something behind. I wanted to deliver it to you personally.'

He dug into his deep pockets and pulled out our carved wooden Gran-Angel.

I gasped. In all the excitement and upset following the final challenge, neither Gramps nor I had noticed that we hadn't brought Gran-Angel home. I took it into my hands and gave it a little hug.

'Thanks, Santa! It means a lot that you brought this back to us,' I said.

'You know, one special skill that I've gained in this job is that I feel magic in people, places and even objects.' Santa smiled. 'When I touched this angel, I could feel it pulsing – humming and vibrating with Christmas magic. I can tell that a lot of love, kindness and imagination has gone into this. Am I right?'

I nodded.

'I knew it was important that I got the angel back to you, and Santa Mail can be a bit slow around this time of year. They receive a lot of letters, but they don't get much sent out.'

I gazed at Gran-Angel. 'Gramps and Gran used to love Christmas,' I said. 'And I mean *really* love it. Every year they turned their house into this proper winter wonderland. Fairy lights inside and outside, the biggest wreath on the door, Christmas songs playing before breakfast. People from the neighbourhood used to stop by, just to see the decorations. Gramps and Gran made it special for our whole family, and the whole community, especially with all their work on the grotto.'

Once I started talking about Gramps and Gran, I couldn't stop. I told Santa about the Gran-Angel – how years ago Gramps couldn't find an angel decoration that looked like Gran so he'd carved his very own.

'You're right,' I said. 'This angel was made with a lot of love – and it's even more precious to us because Gran's gone now.'

'She sounds like an amazing woman,' said Santa.

I smiled. 'She was the best. This is Gramps's first Christmas without her and it's really hard – for all of us, but especially him. I brought Gran-Angel to Christmasland because she would have loved it there.' I paused. 'I could go on . . .'

I could have said that I also wanted Gramps to remember their love and the love he and Gran gave to our family. I could have said that I wanted Gramps to remember that he loved Christmas – but it suddenly felt like too much.

Santa regarded me thoughtfully. As if he didn't need me to speak. 'I'm starting to see why you broke the rules . . .'

I nodded. 'There was no way Gramps would have applied, but I knew he'd be a great Santa.

He's been the Other Father Christmas for years, after all.' I looked at Gran-Angel, and she smiled up encouragingly at me.

I lifted my chin. 'Despite how it ended, I'm super glad that we got to experience Christmasland, and I'm proud of me and Gramps. And he's proud too.' I paused, then said, 'Come and see this, Santa.'

I led Santa round the side of our house and over to our front-room window. Santa peered in and watched Gramps tell my parents all about our adventures.

Gramps was on his feet now, and acting out things that had happened. We couldn't quite make out what they were saying, but at one point it looked as if Gramps was describing the wild reindeer task. He was dancing about the front room and cupping his hands around his mouth, pretending to be singing as loud as he could. Mum and Dad were creasing

up with laughter, but I could see pride on their faces as well.

'It appears that Curtis Merriman really understands how to tell a good Christmas story. He makes it look very easy,' Santa said.

To my surprise, I saw Santa quickly wipe a tear from his eye even as he chuckled. 'You know, Mikey, Santa is important, but so are all those other Father Christmases who turn up at shopping centres and Christmas fairs. They keep the magic going.' Santa sighed deeply. 'I wish I could make him Santa, Mikey. To be honest, your Gramps and Faith were always my favourites. As I told you, I can sense magic in people.'

Lola Faith and Gramps. I had felt it as well. The magic of Christmas was in both of them.

Suddenly I had an idea.

A really good idea.

I explained it to Santa and showed him the poster in my pocket.

'It's a very interesting suggestion, Mikey.' Santa sounded excited. 'We might be able to pull that off.'

He strode to his sleigh in our back garden and I hurried after him.

'Let me make a call to Chief Elf to check,' said Santa. 'Then let's go inside and share your idea.'

I've never seen my mum so star-struck, not even in the photos of that time when Mum got a backstage pass to meet Usher, her favourite singer!

Gramps got to work making more cocoa tea while I led Santa into the front room, where Mum ran around plumping cushions and wiping invisible crumbs off the coffee table. Dad was a lot more chilled and chatted to Santa about how the grotto at the community was going and even asked for some tips.

Eventually we all sat down with slices of Gran's Jamaican fruit cake and more cups of cocoa tea.

'It's great to see you again, Santa,' said Gramps, though his voice held a little surprise in it. 'But what brings you here, to the real world?'

'An angel,' Santa said.

I brought out the Gran-Angel from behind my back.

'We left her in Christmasland,' I said.

Gramps took Gran-Angel in his hands gently and stared in disbelief. He held her close for a moment, then went over to the tree and placed her in her rightful spot at the top.

'You're home now, darling.' He turned to Santa. 'I don't know how to thank you for this. You used some of your magic to come here.'

Santa chuckled. 'Well, this fruit cake is an excellent start,' he replied, his eyes twinkling. He gave a nod towards Mum and Dad. 'Compliments to the chef.'

'We've been doing lots of baking since Mikey and Gramps have been away,' Dad said.

Mum just smiled modestly, but I could already picture her texting every one of her group chats the moment Santa left.

Gramps stayed standing, hands clasped in front of him. 'There's something I need to say.'

We all went quiet, our eyes on him.

Gramps cleared his throat. 'I'll always miss Claudette. That's not going to change – and I don't want it to. But being in Christmasland with Mikey . . . it reminded me of something I'd started to forget.'

He placed a hand gently on his chest. 'Love doesn't disappear when someone's gone. It stays, and you can carry it forward. Use it. Keep building something good out of it. That's how the love carries on – by being there when you try something new.' He gave a small, steady nod. 'Thank you, Mikey, for making sure I always remember that.'

Santa dabbed at his eyes and gave a great sniff. He then reached for his hanky, blowing his nose with dramatic force.

'I always catch a cold at Christmas,' he muttered, before tucking his hanky away. 'Now, Curtis, there's something I want to say too.'

Gramps raised an eyebrow. 'Go on.'

'I want to give you a job. I want to offer you and Faith Diaz the role of Santa.'

Gramps blinked. 'What?'

'Mikey spotted something the rest of us overlooked when he checked the rules of the competition again.'

I took the poster out of my pocket and read out loud: '*The new Santa will be selected from those who have completed all assigned challenges and demonstrated adherence to the rules of the Santa Search. The new Santa must reflect the values of the role in conduct, character and spirit throughout the course of the competition.*'

Santa grinned. 'As Mikey explained it to me, it doesn't say Santa *has* to be one person. Only that the Santa chosen must have done all the tasks and followed the rules. But if one person didn't do those things . . . and two people together *did*, then technically they've met the criteria to be Santa. Just not in the way anyone expected.'

Dad turned to me, surprised. 'Mikey, I didn't know you were so good at reading contractual clauses!'

I shrugged – I'd learned a lot in Christmasland. 'Chief Elf told us that we need to pay attention to the small details,' I said.

Gramps was shaking his head. 'I don't know what to say.'

'Say yes, Curtis,' Santa replied. 'And then let's go and convince Faith. Between the two of you, all the challenges were completed.' He paused. 'OK, the Kringle Town challenge was cut short due to the Buckles' cheating, but that wasn't your

fault. You did everything correctly in that, and you were still in the game up to the end. Also, Chief Elf confirmed that Faith didn't break any rules, intentionally or unintentionally'.

'I've never heard of the Santa job being shared before,' Gramps said.

'Neither have I,' admitted Santa, 'but there's no rule against it. And, right now, I think Christmas needs both of you. Different strengths. Good hearts. The world is complicated and the job can be very lonely.'

Gramps was quiet for a moment, then his gaze flicked to Gran-Angel on the tree.

At last, he said, 'I suppose it makes sense that my first Christmas without Claudette wouldn't follow the usual script.'

Santa smiled. 'So? What do you say?'

Gramps glanced at me, then back to Santa.

'I say YES.'

27

I**T TURNED OUT THAT CHIEF ELF MIGHT BE** one of the best party planners ever. Who knew he liked to dance so much! He'd organised a huge celebration back in Christmasland for me, Ella and the new Santa, aka Gramps and Lola Faith.

The village square was glowing with more lights than ever, strung into pretty mistletoe shapes. A giant banner hung in the air, declaring:

CONGRATULATIONS TO OUR NEW SANTAS!

Right after Gramps had said yes – and we'd all hugged and whooped with joy – the first thing we had to do was visit Singapore. We went straight to the hospital to find Ella and Lola Faith.

By the time we got there, Ella's brother, Erwin, had woken up from his operation. He was tired but smiling, and the doctors seemed pleased – the transplant had been a success. They were also super surprised to have Santa in their hospital.

For Lola Faith, Ella and her parents, I could tell it was as if they had all been holding their breath and now they could let it out. I think that's why Lola Faith said yes to being Santa. She could see that her family were going to be OK. That, and Erwin said it was his Christmas wish that his lola took the job!

Now, back in Christmasland, it felt like the whole place was celebrating with us. Ella and I knew we couldn't stay long – Gramps

and Lola Faith had a lot to do, as did the elves . . . It was Christmas Eve after all. Santa said that it was important, though, that we were there to see the Christmas magic in Faith and Curtis be fully activated so they can be the new Santa.

As we followed Merry into the Decked Halls, rows of cheering elves lined the hallway, blowing vuvuzelas and tossing streamers. They'd swapped their usual hats for shiny party cones, and the hall was filled with music, fairy lights and dancing. 'Rockin' Around the Christmas Tree' blasted through the loudspeakers as elves whirled between long banquet tables stacked with treats.

At the centre of it all was a round table, glowing with Christmas lights and piled high with every dessert imaginable: peppermint cheesecake, reindeer cupcakes, spiced candied pecans, chocolate-frosted orange cake, snowman cookie-dough bites and more.

'Wait,' said Ella, pointing. 'Lola, do you think that's bibingka?'

Lola Faith leaned closer. 'It is. And it looks amazing.'

'We recreated it with Christmasland magic,' said Merry, smiling. 'To make you feel at home – since you'll be spending more time here.'

'It's a Filipino dessert,' Ella explained to me and Gramps, beaming. 'My mum makes it every Christmas. It's a yummy coconutty rice cake – heaven on a plate!'

'And we have Merriman Christmas cake too,' said Merry. 'We got the recipe from your parents, Mikey.'

I reached for a slice just as Chief Elf – or rather *Elvis*, as he insisted on being called – appeared in a bright electric-blue suit and sparkling hat. His smile was wide, his eyes twinkling.

'Congratulations!' he said, shaking Lola Faith and Gramps by the hand. 'We're thrilled to have

both of you join us. You're going to make a wonderful team.'

'Thank you,' said Gramps, grinning.

'I'm looking forward to working with your helpers too: Mikey, Ella – and Erwin, once he's well enough. He'll be welcome here anytime,' said Elvis.

Then, with a flick of his fingers, Elvis conjured up a glowing red-and-gold key and handed it to Gramps and Lola Faith.

'What's that?' I asked.

'Guess,' replied Elvis.

'The key to the restricted section,' said Gramps.

'Where *all* the Christmas secrets are kept,' Lola Faith added.

'Exactly right,' said Elvis. 'It's the control room for the whole kit and caboodle. I think you are both going to love it in there.'

A deep 'Ho ho ho!' rang through the hall. Santa stepped in, dressed in his red suit one last

time, with an I'M RETIRING sash slung across his chest.

'It's quite something in there,' Santa said. He stared round at us. 'Why are we not dancing? We still have an hour or so left to party before we get to work.' He smiled at Lola Faith and Gramps. 'I will stay for as long as you need me, but I know you two were born for this. One chapter ends and a new chapter begins. As it should be.'

Ella rubbed her eyes just as I yawned.

'You tired too?' she said.

I nodded.

She grinned at me. 'Can you believe our grandparents are Santa? It feels like a dream.'

'They're going to be the best team,' I said. 'And we get to help them, and visit Christmasland whenever we like.'

'But how are they going to sort out who does what?' Ella asked.

I shrugged. 'They'll work it out. They're the joint amazingest after all.'

Then I yawned again. Merry had told me this was the biggest celebration Christmasland had seen in decades but all I wanted to do was sleep.

Gramps walked over to me and I leaned against him. He slung an arm around my shoulder and kissed my forehead. I let myself rest for a moment . . .

Then I was blinking, rubbing my eyes as I was startled out of sleep. It was quiet. Still. I was back in my room in Toxteth. The date on my digital clock said the twenty-fifth of December. Christmas morning. But the last thing I remembered was seeing Lola Faith and Gramps transforming into Santa and hearing the cheers of elves. But maybe I had dreamed that – my memories all felt so fuzzy.

I sat up slowly. Had it been a dream? The

Santa Search, the sleigh rides, the wild reindeer and escape rooms. All of it?

I threw off the duvet and ran to the window. The sky outside was a soft, pale grey. No shimmering skies or glowing portals. Only Toxteth rooftops under a fresh coat of snow.

I took the stairs two at a time and skidded into the front room. The tree was lit. Gran-Angel sat on top. My stocking was full. A small card poked out of the top, the paper thick and gold edged.

I pulled it free and read it.

Save a piece of Merriman Christmas cake for me, Mikey Boy. I'll be over this evening. Love, Santa (aka Gramps)

ABOUT THE AUTHORS

SERENA HOLLY is the pen name for the creative partnership of award-winning writers Priscilla Mante and Jasmine Richards for *The Other Father Christmas.*

PRISCILLA is the author of the *Dream Team* series and *Football's Hidden History.* She grew up in Glasgow on a steady diet of books and football, and now lives in England, where she spends her time writing stories for children and adults, travelling and trying out new recipes from around the world.

JASMINE is the author of the *Unmorrow Curse* duology and a screenwriter on *PJ Masks* and *Jo Jo and Gran Gran.* As chief storyteller at Storymix, she has created over twenty-five books for children and teens, including *The Marvellous Granny Jinks and Me* and the *Aziza's Secret Fairy Door* series.

ABOUT THE ILLUSTRATOR

SHAHAB SHAMSHIRSAZ is a children's book illustrator based in Tuscany, Italy. He has loved drawing since childhood and is passionate about bringing stories to life through his artwork. Shahab studied painting at the Academy of Fine Arts and attended a comics and illustration school in Florence. He is especially inspired by fairy tales and folk tales from around the world.

EDITOR'S NOTE

You've just finished reading *The Other Father Christmas*, and I hope Mikey and Gramps's adventure has felt as cosy and warm as your favourite Christmas jumper. This book is extra special because it's the very first story published by Storymix Books. Thank you to everyone who has been a part of making it happen.

We created this story because we noticed something missing. There weren't enough Christmas tales that showed all kinds of families and traditions. We wanted to change that and invite everyone to our festive party of words and pictures!

Maybe Mikey's journey reminded you of your own family, or helped you imagine how children all around the world celebrate at this time of year. If this story gave you new ideas or questions, we'd love for you to share them with the people you care about, or even with us at Storymix Books.

Thank you for joining us for this very first adventure. We're proud and glad that we get to share this moment with you.

The Editor,
Storymix Books